Elbridge Streeter Brooks, W. T. Smedley

In Leisler's times

An historical story of Knickerbocker New York

Elbridge Streeter Brooks, W. T. Smedley

In Leisler's times
An historical story of Knickerbocker New York

ISBN/EAN: 9783744722995

Printed in Europe, USA, Canada, Australia, Japan

Cover: Foto ©Andreas Hilbeck / pixelio.de

More available books at **www.hansebooks.com**

IN LEISLER'S TIMES

AN HISTORICAL STORY

OF KNICKERBOCKER NEW YORK

BY

E. S. BROOKS

Author of "In No-Man's Land," "Historic Boys," etc.

TWENTY-FOUR ILLUSTRATIONS BY
WILLIAM T. SMEDLEY

BOSTON
LOTHROP, LEE & SHEPARD CO.

PREFACE.

Every town has its history, and, whether written or un-written, every town has its romance also. In many a musty old chronicle and many a dry-looking documentary record lie rich historic facts and seeds of romance.

As each year, our country grows farther away from its beginnings, the thronging incidents of the present crowd out, especially from young minds, the privations and struggles of the past. Not a boy or girl who now walks the splendid streets of New York thinks of the days when the great city was in its infancy, or of the boys and girls of that olden time, to whom life was just as sweet and joy-filled as it is to the bright young people of to-day.

It is to afford a scanty glimpse of those far-off days, and of the real boys and girls who then romped and chatted in the little Knickerbocker town that this book has been written.

More than this, it is an attempt to reclaim from unmerited oblivion the name and character of one of America's earliest, stanchest and most unselfish patriots—Jacob Leisler, Lieutenant Governor of the Province of New York, the first representative of the American people and one of the remote causes of American independence.

Histories and cyclopædias alone give him scant mention, if any. His motives have been questioned, his character assailed, and his work belittled. But, beneath all the dry and wordy records of his times there breathes a spirit which even the quaint spelling and tediousness of the old documents cannot obscure — the spirit of resistance to tyranny, of devotion to duty, of cheerful service for others, of a manly and courageous stand for honor, for justice and for right.

If this chapter in the history of old New York shall interest young readers in the life-work of a noble man and in the home scenes of a great city in its "day of small things," the author will feel amply repaid for thus introducing the boys and girls of to-day to their young forefathers of two hundred years ago.

E. S. B.

CONTENTS.

CONTENTS.

CHAPTER XIII.

IN LEISLER'S TIMES.

CHAPTER I.

IN THE DOMINIE'S ORCHARD.

WITH puff and snort, high in air like a railroad on stilts, the dummy-drawn cars of the New York Elevated Railroad steam through the city streets. From Harlem Bridge to the historic Battery they dash on — past brownstone front and towering apartment-house, past open park and high hotel, past crowded tenement and whirring factory and dingy dwellings of the swarming poor, now under the great bridge, and now in sight of the busy river and the sister city upon the further bank, until at last they whizz past blocks of warehouses and, spanning the open square and the trim grass plots of Battery Park, stop at the ferry slips close to the water's edge.

Well — just about where now the "L" road steaming away from the busy Fulton Street Station gives us, looking out of the broad car windows, a peep through long rows of high-walled buildings to the brown front of old St. Paul's and the rush and crush of Broadway — two healthy and happy-faced children walked in the bright sunshine of an April morning two hundred years ago, beneath the spreading branches of the big apple-trees in what was then known as the Dominie's Orchard, beyond the city walls.

A brisk, southeasterly breeze, strong with the sea-smell it had brought with it across the white-capped bay, played through the faintly-greening apple-boughs. An adventurous robin, bound to have a long and busy summer, poured out a flood of song from a swaying branch, while, strolling contentedly beneath the trees, three comfortable-looking cows nibbled the fresh spring grass, and blinked their big brown eyes in serene appreciation of the fact that their lines had fallen unto them in so pleasant a place as the Dominie's Orchard in the bright April weather of the year of grace, 1689.

And, as the cows thought, so too thought the children, bright young people in their early teens, as in the quaint boy and girl costumes of the old Dutch days they sauntered on beneath the apple boughs. Indeed the young girl seemed in a merrier mood than usual and her clear, ringing laugh was so full of fun that it caused even Mr. Robin Redbreast to break off his song and look down in surprise upon his seeming rival.

"No, no, Ab'm," golden-haired Mary Leisler cried in high glee, "you have not caught it yet. You will never learn the right of it, will you? Now mark me: rullities * — rutler-chers, 'tis, and not *reau-la-chez*, as you would say it."

"A plague upon my French tongue, then," said her companion with an impetuous boyish gesture. "But, sure, *belle* Marie, how may you expect me to give the true Dutch turn to all your dreadful words?"

"Dreadful, say you, Ab'm?" exclaimed the girl.

"Ay, dreadful, said I, Marie," the boy replied.

---

* Roltetje or rullities: a favorite old Knickerbocker tidbit, composed of pressed beef and tripe, soused in spiced vinegar and cut into small and appetizing slices.

" So dreadful that I must fain be ever murdering them as you do see.   Now this — what call you it ? — *reau* — "

" Rul — rul," prompted Mary, slowly, " rul-ler-chers — "

" That you are trying to teach me," he went on, scarce heeding her correction; " I never may compass that."

" Nay," broke in the laughing girl, but you can compass the rullities themselves full easily, and that know I.   Come now, Ab'm, how large a share did you compass this morning ? "

" Why — not so vast a lot, Marie," he replied, " but then — you know — your mother doth make them marvellously good-tasting."

" And you have a marvellously good stomach for them too,"said the girl.   " But then," she continued, "that is nothing strange. You have the same for all our home dishes.   Why, Ab'm, you are more Dutchman than Frenchman anyhow."

" And why not, *belle* Marie," answered the lad with true French courtesy. " When the poor Huguenots were driven from home, who was it welcomed

and cared for them but the good Dutchmen of Holland and the better ones of New Amsterdam — or New York as we call it since the English took the town ? "

" Ay, but if the story goeth rightly, Ab'm," said young Mistress Mary, " we of New York did scarce treat you generously."

" 'Twas but your law, Marie," young Abram Gouverneur responded. "The Heer Van Cortlandt could not change the law for our sakes even though we were gentle of blood and birth. If your laws say that paupers who may not have withal to pay their passage-fees, or port-charges, must be sold for the city's benefit, why, sold they must be, I suppose ; and but for your good father —"

" O, yes, tell me about it, do, Ab'm," said the girl, full of interest ; "tell me about it pray, for my father never will."

" ' Tis but like him to keep his own good deeds dark," said the lad gratefully. " But thus it was : Five years back when the great king Louis drove my father and the rest of the Huguenots from France, we followed the throng to Holland. But

we were sore beset upon the way, robbed and maltreated, and then my father died of the fever. My
mother and I strove on until we reached Amsterdam,
but when we were come there, lo, her father, Heer
Patem, the captain, with whom we looked to find
a haven, was dead also. Then we turned our eyes
across the seas hoping to find a quiet home in a
new land, but, ere we might get away, a rascal law-
man cheated my mother of what little she had left,
and when the ship sailed from Holland, we had not
a guilder to our names. So we were fain to come here
as refugees, and when we were landed at the Water
Gate, the Heer Van Cortlandt said that being pau-
per-refugees we must even be sold as vagrant persons to pay the ship's charges and the port-dues."

"Dreadful!" exclaimed sympathetic young Mistress Mary.

"My mother pleaded hard," continued Abram.
"She showed the papers of her goodman, my father,
and those of her father, Heer Patem, the captain.
She told how we were of gentle birth and how my
father's forefathers had fought for the religion at
La Rochelle and Ivry. But it availed us nothing

until your father pushed his way through the prees, and said he would be foul craven and falser Christain did he stand by and see the daughter and the widow of a brave Huguenot soldier sold like to a black Barbary negro-man. And then did he redeem us by himself paying the ship-master and the haven-master their charges, and so gave us our liberty. And, do you know, *belle* Marie, I really think I do remember that he did fillip his fingers in the Worshipful Heer Van Cortlandt's face when it was all over, and cry him shame for such a soulless deed."

" I'll warrant me he did," said Mary Leisler solemnly. "For, truth to say, my father feareth no man from Garry Teunisson, the town constable, to the King's High Majesty. And do you know," she continued, lowering her voice to a still more solemn whisper, " I do myself esteem the Heer Van Cortlandt as a most mispleasing man, even though he be my high and mighty cousin and the Mayor of the town. Why, Ab'm, he bade me be gone from the green behind the Stadt Huys * one day, and said that

---

* The Stadt Huys, or State House, was New York's first City Hall.

maids who knew not how to keep at home should be made to learn the how of it !   Ugh — hateful old thing.   As if Getty* Van Cortlandt was not quite as bad as I — yes, and worse !" with which rather illogical conclusion Mistress Mary's face flushed with indignation as she recalled the Heer Van Cortlandt's words of censure.

"And I can cry you 'yes' and 'amen' to that, Marie," young Abram chimed in.   "For the Heer Van Cortlandt doth not love me overmuch, as I do know.   And, truth to say, I have grown to fear him too.   For — " and here Abram looked around somewhat cautiously — "I much suspect that he doth deem me to have had some hand in the slipping off his periwig in the church last summer. You mind it, do you not, Marie?"

Did she not, though ! As if any little lady in her mischief-loving teens could ever forget such good cause for laughter.

"Why, Ab'm," she said, "if it had not been that my mother had laid her hand right heavily upon my mouth, I should have laughed aloud in the

* Getty — Gertrude.

church." And you fun-loving boys and girls can scarcely appreciate the awfulness of such a crime two hundred years ago. "O, did you have a hand in it, though ?" she asked, now full of curiosity.

The graceless young refugee laughed a sly little laugh. " 'Twere better not to drive me too closely, *belle* Marie," he said, "for, true, I dare not say. 'Twas thought, you know, that some imprisoned pitch did ooze from out the pine back-board with the undue heat, and that the Heer Van Cortlandt's periwig was caught by that, and — well, 'twere best for all to think so yet. Leastways, 'twere best for Jacob, Jr., and for me, that all *did* think so."

" Ah, ha," said the girl with freshly roused suspicions, "then did my torment of a brother have part in it, too ? But, sure, why did I not think of that ? I'll warrant me there's no mischief afloat that he hath not — ah — why, hark ! What may that be, Ab'm ? "

And as upon the children's ears there came through the mass of apple boughs a sudden cry for help, they stopped short and peered before them in some surprise and doubt. Again the cry came.

The robin broke off his flood of song and flew away dismayed. The cows stopped in their grazing, sniffed the air suspiciously, gave a low *moo-oo* of curiosity, sniffed the air once more and then turned tail and galloped clumsily townward. But Abram started in the direction from which came the cry for help followed hard by Mary. "What can it be?" he said.

CHAPTER II.

UP IN THE APPLE BOUGHS.

A S the children hurried on, again came the cry for help, and now Mary, clinging to Abram's arm, strove to hold him back.

"No, no, Ab'm," she said, "do not go. It may perchance be trouble or even worse danger."

"The more cause then for me to be on hand," said the lad. "If there be danger afoot it is for me to help and not to run away. Keep you close to me, Marie, and 'twill perhaps be safer than if I left you here or sent you back alone." And clasping her hand fast, the boy caught up a broken apple bough from the ground and hastened in the direction from which came the redoubled shouts.

"Ah, good youth, brave youth," sounded a pleading voice from somewhere amid the tree-tops, "hasten quickly, I pray, and free me from this ravening beast, who like Satan goeth up and down seeking whom he may devour. See! see, good youth, kind youth, here am I imprisoned in this scarce comfortable tree-crotch!"

Still unable to see anything for the mass of branches, even though yet leafless, the children looked up and around, when suddenly Mary's mingling exclamation of surprise and amusement told that she had lighted upon the owner of the mysterious voice.

"Look, look there, Ab'm!" she cried. "See, in the Dahrklaashaa to the right! 'Tis the stranger gentleman; 'tis the English dominie from the fort. And O, look, look, down below him! Why, Ab'm, he's treed by a bear!"

And Mary was right; for there, almost from the tip-top of the big Dahrklaashaa apple-tree, a troubled and appealing face, with spectacles astride of nose and a ministerially clothed neck, looked down upon the two young people, while not a half-dozen branches below him, and looking upward at his clerical companion, squatted the cause of the frantic cry for help — a big brown bear, blinking his vicious little eyes and wagging his head from side to side in the restless manner peculiar to bears, as if in high enjoyment of his gigantic joke in thus so successfully treeing the English parson in the Dominie's orchard.

Nimble young Mary, trained in woodland ways, climbed a neighboring tree and, perched upon a swaying bough, settled herself to see the fun, while Abram, glancing up through the branches, called out reassuringly to the terrified parson: "Hold you fast, sir; hold you fast and fear not. These sort of bears be harmless unless you do anger them or seek to steal their cubs. He thinks perchance you have something sweet or toothsome about you which he may nose out —"

"Nay, good youth," returned the beleaguered parson, "I have naught toothsome about me save my discourse on Sanctification."

Abram cast aside his cap and blouse and saying, "Keep you fast to that limb, sir, I will be with him anon," he "shinned" up the tree and, still grasping his broken bough, worked his way out upon a neighboring branch, so as to face the

big brown fellow who blinked away in evident perplexity as to the intentions of this new-comer.

"You disrespectful beast," said young Abram,
regarding the bear severely. "Where be your
manners that you thus discommode our stranger
guest — and a dominie at that? You should be
drawn and quartered for so foul discourtesy had
I but gun and knife along."

The bear looked across at the young lecturer
and, with a surly growl, backed slowly out towards
the end of the limb. Abram kept pace with him
and, clinging with one hand to the limb above, he
lifted his stick with the other and fetched Mr.
Bruin a stinging thwack across his clumsy paws.

"Get you down, get you down, sir," he cried,
punctuating his sentences of reproof with rousing
thwacks. "You are no better — *thwack* — than a
misbelieving pagan — *thwack* — or a churchless
pirate — *thwack* — who hath no respect for worthy
dominies or their precepts — *thwack* — *thwack!*
Get you down, I say — *thwack* — and learn to
treat your betters — *thwack* — *thwack* — with more
courtesy — *thwack* — *thwack* — *thwack!*"

MAYOR VAN CORTLANDT HAS A FALL.

The bear growled in protest at his punishment, pulling up first one belabored paw and then the other to dodge the storm of blows. He strove to get at the nimble lad, but wise young Abram had calculated his chances and kept just beyond the reach of the brown bear's clumsy paws and his long and threatening claws.

"How is it with you, good youth?" came the quavering query from the parson in the tree-top. "Is the ravening beast yet quelled, or doth he still incontinently rage and resist?"

"Faith, reverend sir," replied the boy; "he seemeth not to like his chastisement, but danceth up and down like to a lad with thistles in his hose. He hath, I think, learned the error of his ways by this and would gladly climb aloft and beg your reverend pardon—if so be you wish to have him do so."

"I give it him—I give it him. Let him not come aloft, I pray," exclaimed the uneasy parson. And Abram, smothering a laugh, rained now such a new and vigorous shower of blows upon poor Bruin's paws that the badgered beast could stand it no longer, but with a final growl dropped heavily to the ground and shambled surlily away, much to the surprise and discomfort of two stately gentlemen who were walking in earnest conversation under the spreading apple boughs in the Dominie's Orchard. Indeed, so disconcerted were both these stately gentlemen by the unexpected apparition of a big brown bear making towards them, that one of them backed hastily against a sturdy tree-trunk and crying "Avaunt, Satanas!" struck at the beast with his stout cane as a defence, while the other, equally surprised, started to get out of the bear's path so hastily that he took no heed as to his steps and, catching his foot in an uncovered apple-root, fell heavily to the ground where he lay bawling lustily for help, convinced that the bear had pounced upon him. The bear, poor fellow, feeling that he had gotten into most unfriendly society where his room was plainly more desirable than his company, shambled rapidly out of sight, and Abram and Mary, descending from their respective perches in the Dahrklaashaas, saw to their dismay that the stately gentleman who now lay sprawling beneath the apple-trees was none other than the one whom they both held in so much awe — the Worshipful Heer Van Cortlandt, Mayor of His Majesty's loyal city of New York and member of the Governor's Council.

CHAPTER III.

A RUFFLED DIGNITARY.

IT was almost too much for young Abram Gouverneur's ready sense of the ludicrous to see the Worshipful Member of the Governor's Council frantically clawing the ground to escape the clutches of the bear, and shouting lustily for help meanwhile. Sweet Mistress Mary's mischievous laugh came rippling out right heartily when she saw that the bear was making off as fast as his clumsy legs could carry him, and that the Worshipful Member of the Governor's Council was really more scared than hurt. It is but a step, you know, from the sublime to the ridiculous even when bears are after you.

But a man who is over-solicitous as to his own dignity can never appreciate a joke which in any degree ruffles that same dignity, and the Heer

Van Cortlandt, instead of looking upon the comical side of the affair, rose from the ground angered at the bear, angered at himself, and especially angered at the two young people who had been witnesses of his most undignified position. But, when he heard the young girl's merry laugh and saw that the bear had really fled from the field, his anger grew still more hot. His face was flushed with rage, and as he saw Abram running to his assistance he broke out passionately:

"So; it is this graceless young varlet, is it, that turneth brute bears loose into Christian boundaries to take his betters unawares? This is not the first time you have gone such a gait, young sir "—and he flourished the cane which Abram had picked from the ground and handed him, full in the lad's puzzled face—"not the first time, young sir; but, good faith, I shall see to it that it be the last. Trust me, but I will see if such scapegrace tricks as these shall go unpunished. If your patron and my—pho!—most worthy cousin, Jacob Leisler, cannot teach you manners, then will I try what the prison stocks and the—"

Justice-loving young Mary could no longer stand this most unwarranted attack upon her playmate.

"O no," she broke in impetuously, laying her hand upon the worshipful and wrathful counsellor's arm, "good cousin — Van Cortlandt —" she spoke the words rather hesitatingly, "you are altogether wrong.   Ab'm did not —"

But the angry man would have none of her.

" And you too," he exclaimed, rudely throwing off her hand ; "you too, a saucy young baggage, to laugh in my face, forsooth, and tell me I am wrong! Where be your manners, child?   Is the respectfulness of this good city all gone astray, that the very children browbeat their elders and fling words at their betters?   Were it but old Governor Stuyvesant's day you should both know what it meant to contradict and laugh at a *schepen* of the city !"

By this time the imprisoned parson in the treetop had descended from his perch in the Dahrklaashaa, while the Dutch dominie had recovered his wits and left the secure backing of his treetrunk.   As they approached the little group they caught each other's hands.

"Ach, so! 'Tis good Dominie Woolley," cried Dominie Selyns, the Dutchman; and, "why, bless me! 'tis my worthy brother Selyns," cried Parson Woolley, the Englishman.

" And did you too face the bear, good brother?" asked Dominie Selyns.

"Not I indeed, my brother,"said Parson Woolley. "Good faith, he would have left but little face on me, I fear, had it not been for this worthy youth here, who clomb the tree and drove the monster off. But what is awry here? The Worshipful Mr. Van Cortlandt seemeth angered. What hath the lad done?"

"O, sir," cried Mary appealingly, as the parson and the dominie approached, "you can tell the Heer Van Cortlandt how Ab'm had no hand in turning the bear into the orchard, can you not?"

"Why, that can I, fair mistress," the fussy little parson replied. And then buttonholing the still ruffled Member of the Governor's Council, he dropped into a long story of how he was walking out into the Dominie's Orchard to smell the early spring and find a theme for his next Sabbath Day's discourse at the Fort, and how he encountered the unmannerly brute of a bear coming towards him under the apple-trees.   How that, not knowing the nature of the beast, he was sore affrighted, and hastily clomb the apple-tree for safety, and how, good sooth, he heard something scratching below him and, lo! there was Master Bruin scrambling up after him.   How, thinking he was destined to be less fortunate than the Prophet Daniel in the den of lions he trembled in terror at his possible fate; and how when he could neither dislodge the brute, nor drive him away, he had clambered into the very topmost branches of the tree and called out lustily for help.   "Whereupon," said the good parson, "this worthy youth hearing me hasted instanter to my aid, and hammered upon the brute beast's paws right valiantly until he loosened his hold and tumbled him down to the ground, where, unfortunately, he seemeth to have encountered you, Worshipful sir, and given you a fright and a fall as well.   I marvel much that your goodly town suffereth such ravening beasts to be at large so nigh the city gates. But then," he continued, linking an arm into that of each of his companions, " what better can we expect of pagan brutes when such wild beasts of doctrine as I do find here among you — Labadists and Quakers and all such — prowl about and devour the good seed which — "

But long before the English parson had dropped into fierce theological debate with the equally obstinate Dutch dominie, the children had left them far behind, glad to escape from the Worshipful Counsellor's wrath, and hurrying back towards the city, through the clover pastures and across the Maiden's Lane, were soon within range of the palisadoed wall of the little city, which guarded it against attack from the north and stretched across the island from about where Wall Street now running eastward from the river, brings up against the steepled front and crumbling gravestones of old Trinity.

As they ran down the steep hill that sloped to the shore just above the Water Gate, they heard and soon spied a noisy crowd gathered around the porch of the vrouw Annekin Litschoe's tavern just within the Water Gate. True to the nature of children, from the year one until now, Abram and Mary pushed their way into the press to learn what all the talk was about.

"What can be astir, Ab'm?" asked Mary, fully as inquisitive as he.

"Something, sure," replied the lad, "but just what it may be I cannot make out." Then catching sight of a youthful acquaintance and a kindred spirit wedged in the throng ahead of him, Abram clutched him with the grip of boyish determination and called out: "Hoi; say; Barry, Barry Van Schaick! What's astir?"

But young Barent Van Schaick was a late arrival too, and his answer was confused and unsatisfactory.

"I don't know, Ab'm," he said, throwing a backward glance at his questioner. "I hear them talking about Frenchmen and Papists and Injuns and Yankees and something about the King's Majesty being fled and — what may that be? why — Governor Andros is hanged in Boston town!"

"O, never, surely!" exclaimed Abram, all excitement and incredulity at this last piece of news. "Who sayeth that?"

"Who sayeth it?" echoed Barry, craning his supple neck and jumping up to look across the throng of wagging heads, "why, who should say it but him who should know it? Cannot you see — 'tis John Perry, the post-rider, just in from Boston town!"

Sure enough; there he was — John Perry the post-rider. Not all the king's horses nor all the king's men could keep the young folks back now.

For a wonderful man to all the boys and girls of old New York two hundred years ago was this same John Perry, the post-rider. A wonderful man, greater and more important almost than the King's Deputy himself — the bewigged and belaced Lieutenant Governor, Mr. Nicholson, who lived in the big house by the Fort. For John Perry, the post-rider, was of hale and hearty English build, fleet rider and firm friend to all the children on his long route. Every other Wednesday he came spurring through the city gate bearing letters and despatches from Hartford and the Boston colony and far-off Pemaquid, and happy the boy who could hold the post-rider's panting horse as, his despatches delivered at the Stadt Huys, he dismounted and sat awhile in buff jerkin and slouch hat upon the stoop of the vrouw Litschoe's tavern, just within the Water Gate, full of the latest gossip and the cheeriest jokes. And, next to the post-rider, the boy who could hold the post-rider's fretting horse, was the hero of the hour and the envy of his fellows.

Over the heads of their elders there came to the children scraps of the post-rider's talk.

"Not possible, Ryck Crueger?" they heard him exclaim, a trifle testily. "Why, who should know better than I? I tell you, man, here be lively times a-coming for your sleepy Dutchdom of Manahadoes. For, hark you, as surely as I sit here, the Worshipful Governor Andros is in Boston gaol; King James is run away to the French frog-eaters; the Munseers are on the sea steering straight for Sandy Hook and your shaky little fort yonder, and the Prince of Orange is King in London!"

Here was news enough for one day surely; and as, soon after, they wriggled out of the crowd, not caring to listen to the long-winded discussion of the political situation and the varying opinions as to which was the rightful monarch — James the old

King or the young Stadtholder, William, the Prince of Orange — Barry Van Schaick cried out in his usual happy-go-lucky way: "O, who careth who may be the king? It's puncheons and tar barrels any way they put it; so huzzoy for a rouse! For, see you not, Ab'm, whether John Perry speaks the truth or no, we'll have the fire alight down by the old horse-mill as soon as the dark cometh? Either way, I tell you. For, if so be that King James be yet king, it's puncheons and tar barrels for very joy at his victory over the pestilent rebels! But if the Prince of Orange be king indeed, as John Perry doth say, why, then, Ab'm, 'tis victory for the other side! And so it's tar barrels and puncheons and a royal rouse either way."

And the young philosopher swung his cap and cut a caper in anticipation of his jolly bonfire in honor of the king — which king in no wise mattered. So, you see, the spirit that in our own time sets the streets of New York ablaze on Election nights, whichever party wins, is as old as the city itself.

CHAPTER IV.

THE bright April day had worn itself well on to afternoon when Abram pushed his head in through the open half-door of the shining Leisler kitchen.   Only his head, please notice, for under no pretence dared he protrude his soiled feet upon that dreadfully clean and freshly sanded kitchen floor.

"Mother Leisler," he said, "Barry and I are going up to goode vrouw Weber's with a roll of mother's '*hoof kaas*.' May not Marie go with us too?"

"Not so, lad," replied Mary's busy mother; "the maid hath been *over-loopen** the town with you far too much already, and she must even bide at home and tax herself with tasks she hath neg-

---

* "Over-loopen" — clambering or leaping over — Dutch for the Yankee "galivanting."

lected. 'There's not a maid on the Strand that is such a wander-foot as she. So go you alone, Ab'm, you and Barry there, and see you mind your manners with your elders. And, *ach, so!* since you are holden for the Fresh Water, why, take ye my greeting too, and this pypkin of *kool-slaa*, like handy lads, to the goode vrouw Weber for me."

Mary's sorely disappointed face troubled Abram, but there was no appeal from the mother's decision in those days, and so the boys trudged off towards the Fresh Water and the goode vrouw Weber's. Now the goode vrouw Weber was quite a character in that quaint old town of two hundred years ago. She was a relic of the times when their High Mightinesses the States General of Holland ruled the province — the days of the Heer Director Kieft and stout old Governor Stuyvesant, and she was full of stories of those stirring times when the city lay all within the boundary of the palisadoed wall, when the Quakers were whipped at the cart's tail through the Winckel Street and the Heerengraaft, and when the Indian savages, full twenty-hundred strong, ran their canoes ashore at Schrey-

er's Hook, where Castle Garden now stands, and
came prowling through the city streets that dreadful September night in the year '56, when they laid
Staten Island all a-waste and murdered every man,
woman and child from Hoboken to Pavonia.   And
as in her clean "fore room " in her low-roofed cottage
by the Kolch or Fresh Water, the goode vrouw would
tell her marvellous tales and would show, above the
ample fireplace, the great "goose gun " that had
belonged to Wolfert Weber, her goodman long since
dead, and would tell how he had shouldered it when
he sailed away with the stout old Governor Stuyvesant against the audacious Swedes at Fort Cas-
imir on the Delaware, and how he had turned out
with the *burger-wagt*, or citizen guard, that dreadful
night when the savages tomahawked the excellent
Heer Van der Grist on the Broad Way, the children's eyes would grow big with interest and wonder until little Mistress Mary would hide her face
in fear, and Abram and Barry, with beating hearts,
would wish that they were men to go off to Fort
Orange and the patroon's country to bring back furs
and trophies, or a long string of Indian scalps.

But to-day they were forced to go without Mary; and Abram was sad and Barry was mad — the latter all the more so because while he had no Mary along to tease (a sore deprivation for him) he had the undesired burden of Mother Leisler's pypkin of *kool-slaa* which he had not bargained for. So he grumbled away at Abram.

"A plague on your fine generalship, say I," he spluttered. "What sort of a Heer Commander will you be to fight the Onondaga savages, Ab'm, that can plan no better than this? But I say," and here his grumbling changed to excitement, "perchance we may play at being Heer Commanders even before we go against the savages, for Patem's Elishamet's Jan * did say to me this nooning that Gysbert Van Cortlandt and the Heer Colonel's son, with some of the other *Jonkheers*,† were minded to burn tar barrels for King James this very night outside the

---

* It was an old Knickerbocker custom, in speaking of acquaintances, to give not their full names, as Jan Ten Eyck, for instance, but to designate them by their parents' names as, so and so, the son of his father's wife. So "Patem's Elishamet's Jan" meant "John the son of Peter's wife Elizabeth;" "Brachie's Cose's Brachie" meant "young mistress Bridget the daughter of James' wife, the goode vrouw Bridget," etc. This custom has not entirely died out in counties where Dutch blood still runs pure.

†*Jonkheers*, Young aristocrats; Heeren 's, or lord's, sons. —

Lant poort * and Jan has ten good fellows will join to scatter the fire or capture the barrels for the Prince of Orange if but you will lead 'em on. So, will you?"

It was a sore temptation and Abram yielded all too readily. "Will I not though, Barry?" he said. "When is it set?"

"Close after sundown," replied Barry. "So let us hurry back from the Fresh Water lest we be not in time for the fray."

Up the Strand and through the half-ruined Water Gate, under the apple boughs of the Dominie's Orchard, and along the Cripple Beach, across the Smit's Vly, and by the Great Kill, and so on to the Fresh Water, the boys hurried and soon had "made their manners" and given their offerings to the goode vrouw Weber in her neat little cottage by the Kolch, or Fresh Water, which, deep and clear, sparkled in the spring sunlight, where now rises grim and gray and dismal the gloomy prison of the great city — the terrible Tombs. For in those days the Kolch, or Versch Water, as this fresh

**Lant poort* — Land Gate in the old Wall — Wall St. and Broadway.

water pond was called, was away out of town, quite in the country — the "*buyten luyden*" or suburbs of the little Dutch city.

For three pleasant hours did the garrulous goode

AT THE GOODE VROUW WEBER'S.

vrouw Weber hold the two lads spell-bound by the magic of her stories of the old New Amsterdam days; and the afternoon sun was "well on its way to

Paulus Hook," when they struck across the Kolch fields and started for the town by the shortest cut. A bowl of the goode vrouw's "suppawn and malk "* had, however, taken off the keen edge of their appetites and they were full of the spirit of bravery which brave tales always leave with wide awake lads.   Visions of wolves and Indians, of French and Swedish foes, of deep forest trapping and the hunting of bear and beaver, elk and deer, filled their young brains and kept their tongues a-wagging, when suddenly, as they hurried down the hill beyond the Cripple Beach and headed for the Water Gate, they spied Mary running across the little dip of land to meet them.

"The mother said I might," she announced, "and, O Ab'm, what do you think ? Here is more news ! I heard Joost Stoll tell the mother that — what should be that funny sailor's name — that half Yankee who did take us elft-fishing † last year —? "

"Ach ! she meaneth Zagharia Whitspain, Ab'm," said Barry.

"Yes, that is he," Mary said ; "well, Joost says

* Mush and milk — hasty pudding.   † Shad-fishing.

he is just in with his ketch from the Lord Baltimore's patent* and that he did say too that the old King is fled and that he is coming with the French ships and sailor men to the Hoofden.† O, will they come, Ab'm, think you? And what will they do?"

"Why, skin us and eat us, of course, if frogs be not forthcoming," said mischievous Barry Van Schaick. "That's what the Munseers live on, is it not, Ab'm? But then, never you mind, Mary," he said as the maiden's eyes opened wide in surprise and dismay. "We be all right. For, good faith, we know where there be frogs in plenty, do we not, nigh to the old Governor's bouwerie? We will give them all the frogs they want and thus shall save our skins."

"O but I hope they won't come till August," began Mary solemnly, "for then the frogs are big and fat—" when suddenly Barry broke in with:

"So ho; yon cometh Gys Van Cortlandt! Folk do say, Ab'm, that his father, the Heer Mayor, is a rank Papist and cleaveth to King James."

"What, the Heer Van Cortlandt!—and he my

* Maryland.   † The Narrows.

mother's cousin ?   O, Barry, that cannot be," exclaimed Mary.

"Can it not then ?" Barry retorted. " Ask young
Gysbert and see if it is not."

" Indeed that will I not," said Mary with the
least toss of her fair head.   " His father did scold
me roundly this very morning and I'll not speak
with him.   Why should I ? "

" To get even with him, Mary girl," Barry quickly
replied.   " Come, I'll give you a help to serve him
out royally," and before Mary could interrupt him
he called out, " Hoi there, Gysbert, Gys Van Cortlandt !   Here's Mary Leisler sayeth you are to be
laid by the heels in the prison stocks for being
King James' man — you and all your kin ! "

" O, Barry, you know I did not," cried the scan-
dalized Mary.

Gysbert Van Cortlandt turned angrily upon the
three.

" 'Tis like her father's daughter," he answered
with a sneer. " But let her keep her tattling tongue
to herself if she would 'scape the ducking-stool
for a gad-about. 'Tis what she will come to, so

my father sayeth. And he sayeth, too, 'tis sure a sin and shame to see a maid like to her, *over-loopen* so with naught but street boys and pauper slaves — such as he," and he pointed in scorn at Abram.

Mary was aroused in an instant.

"He is no pauper slave, Gysbert Van Cortlandt!" she cried, "and that you know. Abram is as free born a lad as you — and a million times nicer than you and all the lazy *Jonkheers* put together." And Abram's little champion grew quite flushed and excited.

"O, he is, is he, Mistress Niche-Noche?" said Gysbert, contemptuously. "Well, I say he's a low fellow and, good sooth, your father's not much better. My father sayeth 'twas, sure, great pity that our cousin, your mother, did marry such a none-knows-who."

"Ho, my father is as good as your father, any day!" exclaimed indignant young Mary.

"My father's forebears were kings of Courland," boasted Gysbert, "and who were yours? *Ach*. loping louts and you're no better."

Abram could stand it no longer.

"See here, Gysbert Van Cortlandt," he cried hotly, facing the lad angrily, "keep your nicknames for your fellows and not for your betters, or 'twill be the worse for you. You may say what you please about me, but if you dare say aught against my good patron, the Heer Leisler, or his daughter, *la belle* Marie, I'll make you rue your words full solemnly, trust me but I will."

"O, will you though," snarled Gysbert, who was fully a head taller than Abram and something of a bully as you see. "I'll say what I please, Heer Galley-slave, Heer Pauper, and you shall not say me nay. You're a flout, and he's a lout, and she's a pout, and here's a clout to cap my rhyme withal!" And without an instant's warning he fetched Abram so sounding a cuff upon the side of his head as sent the lad staggering.

Abram's hot French blood was up in an instant. Breaking loose from Mary's restraining grasp, he dashed upon Gysbert with such vehemence that had the bigger lad not taken to his heels at once he would have fared badly. Up and down the open space that stretched without the Water Gate they raced and chased and dodged, while young Barent Van Schaick, who had caused all the mischief, fairly hugged himself with delight, and anxious-faced Mary watched the race doubtfully.

Down the slope from the city came two sedate gentlemen, passing from the Stadt Huys to the Water Gate to examine the condition of the defences near the Ferry stairs. Wary-eyed Barry scented danger as he saw them coming and was off in a flash. But the race of the combatants went headlong on, and the newcomers were not noticed. Suddenly Gysbert tripped and fell. Abram was close upon his heels, and dashing hard after him, with lowered head, heedless of what was before him, he butted full and heavily against the be-laced waistcoat of the portlier of the two sedate gentlemen and was brought suddenly to a standstill with a firm hand grasping his loosened collar.

" *Ach;* pouf ! how now, how now, young donner-head," cried his captor, with difficulty recovering from the shock of collision. "What means all this riot ? Whom have we here ? "

" More brawling among our lads ? " exclaimed his

companion. "'Tis high time this scandalous — what? Why? — Bayard — as I live, 'tis my lad Gysbert, on the ground, and this young fury — well — body o' me — 'tis that young slave of a pauper Huguenot — 'tis Leisler's potboy. Now, by St. Pol, but this passeth countenance!"

Gysbert picked himself up from the ground, while the Heer Colonel Bayard smiled in spite of himself and the Heer Mayor Van Cortlandt fumed in anger. Then the boy brushed his disordered clothes and said sullenly, "'Twas his fault, father!"

"No word, sirrah! get you home quick," said his father sternly. "And as for you, young jail bird, to the prison stocks and cage you go. Twice now this day have I found you brawling and plotting against your betters. Get you to the constable straight, or I will — but no, I'll not trust you to go. I'll even serve you out myself and break your stubborn naughtiness. Take off your hand, girl," he said angrily, as Mary caught his uplifted arm, "take off your hand, I say, lest you too get your fair deserts."

But ere the upraised cane could fall upon poor

Abram's back, a sudden shadow fell across the group. There was a hurried step, the quick up-stroke of another stout walking-stick, and the descending cane of the Heer Van Cortlandt went whirling from his hands while the Worshipful Councillor himself, starting back in amazement and surprise at this unexpected interruption, looked angrily around to see what intruder could have dared interpose himself between the Heer Van Cortlandt's retributive justice and the trembling culprit.

CHAPTER V.

ON THE STRAND.

YOUNG Abram Gouverneur, too, looked won-
deringly up to see who had interfered to
save him from an almost certain caning at the
hands of the angered Heer Van Cortlandt. But
his curiosity and surprise changed to joy — tem-
pered, perhaps, with a little natural anxiety, for
those were days of stern and severe discipline,
remember — as he recognized, in the grave but determined face of the intruder, his friend and patron,
the Heer Jacob Leisler, Merchant of the Winckel
street, and Captain in the city train-bands.

"What, Leisler! do you dare — " began Van
Cortlandt, fiercely; but the Heer Leisler interrupted him by saying firmly, "'Dare' hath an
ugly sound, friend Stephanus. This lad, as you
know, is under my protection. Trust me but I

will deal justly with him for aught of evil he may have wrought you, but I will esteem myself beholden to you if you will refrain from beatings and threatenings towards him. Now," and he drew Abram to his side and held him firmly there, "what hath he done, I ask?"

"Done?" exclaimed the wrathful Van Cortlandt; "he hath done enough, were he my lad, even, to deserve chastisement, and being as he is but a pauper Huguenot, he merits—"

"Fair and softly, fair and softly, friend Stephanus," again interposed the Heer Leisler in a quiet but determined tone. "False words can never make a foul cause fair. The lad Abram is no pauper Huguenot, as none knoweth better than yourself. His blood is as pure as is yours, Muscovy dukes though your fathers were. So, without more ado, give me, I pray, the evil he may have wrought you, devoid of harsh and hasty names."

"It is not for such as you, Heer Leisler, to tell to me, who am the mayor of your city, how I shall frame my speech," said the Heer Van Cortlandt haughtily. "Nor will the public service permit .

such as I to tarry here bandying words with a
rascal lad like this. Come away, Bayard. But
hark ye, Leisler; I say this boy is a public nui-
sance, and I shall move for his instant punishment
in the stocks and cage if you do not keep him off
the streets. I will have no more brawling in the
public ways." And haughty and heated as ever,
the Heer Van Cortlandt strode after Colonel Bayard through the Water Gate, and on to his big
house by the Water-side.*

As Mary walked cityward between her father
and Abram to her home on the Strand, she gave,
helped out by Abram, a full account of the day's
disturbances and showed her father how wrongly
the Heer Van Cortlandt had judged Abram's
helpful action in the Dominie's Orchard, and his
loyal stand for his patron in the trouble by the
Water Gate. The Heer Leisler admitted the
hastiness of the Worshipful Mayor's conclusions,

---

* Mr. Van Cortlandt's house stood in the Dock Ward, by the Water-
side, at the present corner of Broad and Pearl streets. The Strand, or
Water-side, was the street then fronting the East River, now known as
Pearl street. The streets now lying between Pearl street and the river
were then all under water. Leisler's house stood on the Strand near what
is now Whitehall street.

but as he stood upon the " stoope " of his ugly
stone house on the Strand he said, looking down
upon the lad whom he had befriended, " But mind
you this, Abram, the times are ticklish now and
soon none may know who be friends or foes. I
tell you this because you are a sharp-eyed lad and
can speedily see it for yourself, and because too
you are shrewd enough to note that there is no loss
of love between the Heer Van Cortlandt, or the
Heer Colonel Bayard and myself. See to it, lad,
that you do not by any unwise or hasty action,
fan the fire which needeth now but a little wind
to drive it into a roaring flame."

And as Abram stood at the doorway of his
mother's queer little cottage nearer to the fort he
pondered over the Heer Leisler's charge and said
to himself, " No loss of love, says he? Well, then,
all loss of love, say I. For if, as folk do say, the
Heer Leisler did get the better of those two
grandees among the law-men here, then all the
love that ever was between them must sure be
now clean gone forever. My mother hath told me
that her father, Heer Patem, the captain, oft did

say that when the law is in the love is out. Well,
I'd be right glad, good faith, did they never find
their lost love again. And as for that Gysbert
Van Cortlandt, if ever I get to have another
chance at him, I'll—"and Abram ground his teeth
in a determined and highly improper manner that
boded no good for Gysbert Van Cortlandt, just as
the fleet-footed Barry dashing up to him, said,
"Come on, worthy Heer Commander, the boys
are all waiting for you at the old Horse Mill. We
have Jan Crueger's Jan, and black Cose from the
farm, and big Dirck Ryckman from the Mill, and
the English lad, Tom Allerton, and a lot of others.
With such as they at our back, whom think you
will keep the tar barrels — the *Jonkheers* or our
side?" and seizing Abram's arm he hurried him
up the Strand.

"But why are ye near the Strand, Jan," inquired
Barry as the young conspirators met near the old
Horse Mill. "Here was I telling Ab'm this after-
noon that the fun was to be just beyond the Lant
Poort."

"Why," replied hard-headed little Jan Crueger,

"Tom Allerton heard by the Stadt Huys a while back that the *Jonkheers* had smelled out our plans and would strive to get the better of us by bringing their store of barrels on the Strand here. So I gathered the lads instanter and here be we on the ground before them. But they will be here anon with all their spoil of barrels, and then cometh our chance. Ho, see; yon cometh Teuny Fever-foot with news of them, I'll wager a ducatoon."

As he spoke there came hurrying towards them the Miller Ryckman's little Indian slave, who acted as their scout and spy, Teuny Fever-foot, with word of the enemy's approach. In an instant every mother's son of them scattered for convenient hiding, and not one was in sight when Gysbert Van Cortlandt and Colonel Bayard's son, with a dozen of their natural enemies, the *Jonkheers*, appeared upon the scene with a fine store of tar barrels and one big wine puncheon, which Abram at once recognized as from the store yard of the Heer Leisler's warehouse in the Winckel street.

Very carefully did the new-comers bestow and arrange their material for the proposed bonfire in the open space across the Strand roadway; and then leaving two stalwart guards in charge, they hurried back for other material. But they had barely turned from the Water-side into the shadow of the big houses on the Heeren Graaft, when the lads in ambush sprang from their hiding places, and in a silent sally swooped down upon the guards and the tar barrels, scatteri g the former, and bearing off the latter in noisy triumph up the narrow roadway that ran " *lang de waal,*" on what is now known as Wall street, towards the Land Gate on the Broadway.

But the bewildered sentinels, quickly recovering from their surprise, raised a lusty shout for help with such good effect that soon their own party came racing back from the Heeren Graaft to re-cover their stampeded treasure. Abram and his forces, impeded by the barrels which they were bearing off, could not hope to make rapid head-way and, speedily, pursuers and pursued had met upon the grass-grown ruins of the dismantled palisadoed wall in a fierce contest for the possession of the coveted tar barrels.

"Down with the *Jonkheers!* down with the Papists! down with the grandees!" shouted Barry as, astride a broken line of palisade, he waved above his head a big splinter from the ruined defences, and cheered on the combatants — but shrewdly took no hand in the fray himself. "Hi there, Jan! Jan Crueger!" came his warning, "look out for Sam'l Bayard there; he's rolling away a barrel! Hoi — fen, fen trippings, Gys Van Cortlandt! Look to yourself, Ab'm, or he'll have you down! So; good for you; now then, you Cose, toss the barrel over to Teuny!"

With these and similar remarks Barry helped on the fray, while now and then he would rattle out the couplet caught from some of the Dutch sailors in port —

> *Oranje boven, de Witten onder*
> *Die 't anders meend, die staat der Donder,**

a rhyme from one of the popular songs of the followers of the Prince of Orange.

---

* "The orange's above and the white goes under.
Who says not so shall be shot, by thunder!"

rounding off with the cheer: "Hip huzzoy, for the Prince of Orange! and down with old King James and his frog-eaters!"

But as Barry, from his elevated perch upon the palisade, cheered on the battle, and while neither party appeared to gain the advantage, across from the Stadt Huys and the Strand came the murmur of what must be approaching help or hindrance. The little Indian scout, Teuny Fever-foot, wary-eyed and quick of ear, knew it to be the latter, and his voice rang out shrill and clear above the din of war: "Ho, lads! hoi, masters! 'Ware the Watch —'ware the Watch! Here come the Rattlers!"

Even as he spoke, around from the Strand, and up the Wall street, came hastening the vigilant Rattle Watch, firemen and policemen combined, with the constable of the Dock Ward, Evart Teu-nisson, at its head. And the contending parties of boys, recognizing the approach of a superior power, melted away as quickly as even in these days of our own time a wary crowd of New York boys, waging fierce conflict over election-night

JOOST STOLL.

barrels or the possession of a street will scatter and vanish in an instant at the approach of that blue-coated guardian of the law and enemy of all small boys — the "cop" or "peeler," as above their noise of battle rings the mysterious warning of their scouts: "Lay bones; lay bones. Here comes the cop!"

Only shrewd young Barry Van Schaick was left. For that diplomatic young person, the instant he scented danger, had quietly dropped over the outer side of the ruined wall and, stealing cautiously within its shadow, strolled leisurely down towards the Water Gate and re-entered through that tumble-down gateway, seemingly as innocent of boys and street fights and disputed barrels as if he had just come across lots from the Fresh Water. And while he helped the disgusted Watch gather together the scattered barrels, identifying them from well-known marks, as the property of various worthy burghers of the town, it must be confessed that he slyly appropriated a certain share of the spoils to himself, rolling them, almost under the very noses of the unsuspecting Watch, into convenient hiding-places for future use at his own special bonfire. For Barry was determined to have his jolly blaze, no matter where the Rattle Watch might be, or who, indeed, might be the rightful King of England.

CHAPTER VI.

IN THE MADJE PADJE.

IT was a bright spring morning, some three weeks after the bloodless Battle of the Barrels, that Abram's curly head was thrust in over the open half-door of Mother Leisler's immaculate kitchen and his excited young voice exclaimed, " O, Mother Leisler; here hath come Corny Cortelyou to the Bridge,* saying that Jacob, Jr., did trap a gray wolf in his bear-fall at the *bouwerie* last night, and he bids me come up and help slay him. Yes! and Corny sayeth it is a far bigger wolf than any he did ever see on his grandfather's *bouwerie* at Aquackanonk † —and Jacob, Jr., will

---

*The Bridge across the canal in Broad street was a great place of public resort for men and boys. It was the first Merchants' Exchange or meeting place for the Merchants and was the boys' favorite rendezvous as well.

† Near Newark, N. J.

give me a fourth part of the pelt fee if I will but help him — he did promise me that — and — O — may not Marie come with me too?"

Mary's face glowed with the excitement reflected from Abram's eager eyes and his breezy recital. "O, do, mother," she cried, "do but let me go. Ab'm and Jacob will not let me come to harm."

"Bless the lad," said Mother Leisler as she looked at the flushed faces upturned for her decision. "I do believe me he thinketh more of the pleasure it may give to Mary here than of his share of the pelt fee. And yet, will it be safe? I much fear me, Mary child, lest you may fall into some danger from this ravening beast."

But Abram broke in with fresh protestations and assurances. "And besides," he added as a "clincher" to his plea, "Jacob, Jr., hath the wolf fairly trapped and he could do us no harm surely, if he be in and we be out."

Mother Leisler shook her head in some doubt. "Ay, but wolves get out anon when lads and maids be foolhardy," she said. "But I do know you for a cautious boy, Ab'm," she added; "more so, good faith, than Jacob, Jr., though he be the elder. And sure, how shall a maid be trained in hardiness if she never looketh danger in the face? So get you along to your brother's wolf-trap, child. But as you go, Ab'm, see that you send me Jasper the Najack from the Verlettenberg,* for I need a new gutter above the kitchen here; and stop too, at Baas Claes, the tanner's, in the Madje Padje, and ask his goode vrouw for the nose-cloths† she was to prepare for me, and bid Joost Stoll fail not to keep his word, or my back paths here will go to wrack, all for the want of that load of tan that he did promise me."

Thus weighted with messages, but overjoyed to get off so readily, the happy lad and lassie were soon hurrying up the Strand and over the Bridge to the Verlettenberg in search of Jasper the Najack. That sombre old Indian peddler of bark gutters and firewood was speedily despatched, grumbling at the haste, to Mother Leisler with a

---

* The Verlettenberg afterwards corrupted into the Flattenbarrack, was a hill at the head of the canal in Broad street where the marketmen from Brooklyn and Gowanus brought their stuffs.

† Handkerchiefs.

new bark spout or gutter, to carry off the rainfall
from her kitchen roof, and Mary and Abram, taking a short cut across the "Schaape Waytie" or
Sheep Pasture,* headed straight for "Shoemakers'
Land,"† stopping only at Baas‡ Claes, the tanner's,
in the Madje Padje, or Maiden's lane (now so
broad and busy a city street) to deliver Mother
Leisler's messages to the baas' goode vrouw and
to Joost Stoll.

"Well, well, child," the goode vrouw Fytie (or
Sophie) said, as she bustled out of her little house
near to the tannery, "here's a nice to-do! Here
be my *hokkies* all ready for the turn, and I dare
not leave them. Run you like a good child to
Anatje, the laundry-girl, down at the wash-brook,
and bid her send me the nose-cloths. For she
hath but just now taken them there."

So Mary, with not the best grace, I fear, hurried
down the Madje Padje to the little stream which
the washerwomen used for laundry purposes, while

* Now Broad street near Exchange Place.

† The section now running from Broadway at the Herald Building eastward to William and Gold streets.

‡ Boss or master.

Abram, inwardly chafing at this extra delay, hunted through the tannery in search of Joost Stoll.

Now Joost Stoll was what the boys in these days would call "chief cook and bottle-washer" to the Heer Jacob Leisler — his right-hand man, his "head help" with his merchandise and his belongings, the overseer of his *bouwerie* or farm, and sergeant in his company in the city train band. A grizzled, gruff and burly Dutchman was Joost Stoll, but obliging enough beneath his stolid and somewhat surly exterior — if only "rubbed the right way."

Abram found him in one of the "vile-smelling tan-pits" which were soon after removed to Beekman swamp out of range of the offended nostrils of the growing town, and, still heated from his search, communicated his message in too hurried a manner to mollify the gruff old Dutchman.

" Houf ! take down the tan yourself," he replied, groutily enough. " I cannot do an hundred things, can I ? Nor will I, good faith, while a big loafing lout like to you walketh around an' he were a lazy *Jonkheer* with his orders and his airs. *Saccaremund !* You do not earn your salt, boy ! "

"O, Joost, good Joost!" came a gentle and appealing voice from the edge of the tan-pit, and the grouty fellow softened as he met Mary's appealing eyes.

"Well, nor doth he; doth he, *yung vrouw?* And why should he not take the tan to Mother Leisler himself?"

"Because, good Joost," quoth Mary, "the mother did send the message to you and you alone, and because, moreover, I do want Ab'm to go along with me to help Jacob, Jr., kill the gray wolf he hath trapped in the *bouwerie.*"

Joost Stoll threw up his hands in wonder and climbed out of the tan pit. "Houf, pouf!" he grunted for all the world like a gray wolf himself. "*You* kill the gray wolf — youngsters like you! Well — well — you'll be striving to lead the train-bands next. Hoi; Claes, Claes! did ye but hear that?" he called out to the tanner. "Why, *yung vrouw*, that old Bloody Jaws in the trap will only need to make one bite at the three of ye! Here, you look after the tan, Ab'm, and I will see to the wolf at the *bouwerie.* And, good faith, I must hasten too, or Jacob, Jr., will sure get afoul of the wrong end of the goose-gun and *mün heer* Bloody Jaws will walk out of the trap and pop the lad down his murthering jaws."

A storm of protest from both the young people greeted this unwelcome proposal, and Joost, who spite of his growlings generally let the young folks have their own way, said shortly, as he shouldered his *shoffel*, or scoop, and started off for Mother Leisler's tan, "Well, go your ways and get yourselves in readiness to be *hoof kaas* for the Heer Bloody Jaws. But hark ye, boy," he added in a lower tone, catching Abram by the arm, "the trainbands mean business, and our company do hold the fort to-night. What may hap, may hap. So be you on hand, if you would lend your help."

Abram gave a long, low whistle. Joost Stoll's misty intimations evidently promised a novelty more exciting by far than the killing of the gray wolf at the farm. Perhaps even a row with the Heer Governor himself.

For, though Abram, boy-like, had thought but slightly and cared still less for the storm that was

a-gathering, the little city by the sea was making
history fast through all those fair spring days of
1689. Revolution in England meant confusion in
the colonies, and the people, both those who thought
and those who blindly followed, were beginning
already to clamor for manlier rights and broader
privileges, and to hope dimly for that freedom
which one hundred years later they wrested from
their English rulers. Young people think but little
of politics and public matters save as they promise
visible excitement, or touch their own concerns;
but when once their inquisitiveness is aroused they
are persistently curious and questioning. And so
as this old-time lad and lassie took their way
through "Shoemakers' Land" and toward the
Leisler farm, Mary, who had caught some portion of Joost Stoll's last words, said:

"What is it all about, Ab'm? Why are our
folks so much at work upon the palisadoes and the
wall, and why is my father so forever on the go to
the Stadt Huys, or the fort? Are the Indians
feared? or is it true, as Elsie Straatmaker did tell
me, that the French king is to send shiploads of

murthering Papists here to fry our ears and set us all a-sea from off the Sandy Point?"

"Ho; we would like but to see them try it," said Abram, valiant as any lad — in talk, when danger is remote. "Why, *belle* Marie, no runagate Papist, nor murthering frog-eater, shall fry your little ears while I may be in call. But, truth to say, though, I do not know all the why of this matter; 'tis said, I believe, that it all cometh because the old King James—he who was Duke of York, you know, and for whom our town here is named — hath been driven from England for being a Papist and a cruel-minded tyrant, and because our own brave stadtholder, Prince William of Orange, and his English wife, who is the daughter of old King James, have been made king and queen of England. And some of our folk here are for the one king and some are for t'other. And they do say that old King James doth seek, by help of the French King Louis, whom all good Huguenots hate — ships and soldiers to force us to obey him and not the Prince of Orange who by this day should be king in London town."

"Ships and soldiers!" exclaimed open-eyed Mary, "there; said I not so, Ab'm? Elsie Straatmaker did tell me true that the French King's soldiers would fry our —"

"Ho!" scouted valiant Abram again. "Not while your father is captain in the train-band, and while Joost Stoll is his sergeant and a plenty of brave fellows among us are ready to rush to the walls. Although folk do say, Marie," he continued, "that the Heer Governor Nicholson, in the fort yonder, and his council, your cousin the Heer Mayor Van Cortland, your other cousin the Heer Colonel Bayard and the rich Heer Phillipse of the manor, are all King James' men and secret Papists. But the people — this is what Joost Stoll doth tell me — will have somewhat to say in the matter and will have none of the high and mighty ways of these grandees, but will up and shout hollo! and huzzoy! for our true king, the good stadtholder and his English queen.

"But Ab'm," still persisted the girl, "I cannot well see why we should all be so fluttered and flurried by this trouble between two kings who are so far away. Why may we not stay here all right and quiet, whatever doth happen over-sea, and how is it our concern?"

"O — you would not fathom it even if I should tell you why, *belle* Marie," Abram replied in that lofty and reason-crushing manner with which men —both young and old — usually attempt to dismiss a woman's question on matters of politics. "Maids like you cannot understand such grave affairs."

"But do you, Ab'm?" asked Mary.

"I? Why — of course," replied Abram, confident but confused, "'tis the business of men," and then he was searching for some fresh topic which would allow him to change the subject lest he should be caught tripping, when Mary changed it for him: "O, see ; look there, Ab'm ! Whatever can that mean ? Whatever can be going on ?"

Abram followed her puzzled look, and beneath the chestnut-trees that shaded a little nook just off the narrow path, he saw a sight that caused him also to exclaim hastily, and, drawing back, watch and listen for developments.

CHAPTER VII.

IT was a singularly-assorted company of five that had caused Abram's look of surprise and Mary's startled exclamation. For there, just across the narrow horse-path, gathered within the clump of spreading chestnut-trees, were Gysbert Van Cortlandt and Samuel Bayard, the colonel's son, Teuny Fever-foot, the little Indian slave-boy of Dirck Ryckman the miller, Barry Van Schaick and — Perry the post-rider; the first two appealing, the last one protesting, and the other two unconcernedly stretched on the ground, apparently interested only in an exciting game of "mumblety-peg" or "pick-knife," as Yankee boys call it.

"Nay, but young masters, I may not take the packet," the post-rider was saying as Abram, placing Mary in a safe nook, peered and listened behind his clump of sheltering alder bushes; "ye do know full well that it is worth my office, and mayhap my head, to take such post-matter from aught but the Secretary of the Council, or from their Worships at the Stadt Huys."

"Ay; but do not I tell you, Perry," persisted Gysbert Van Cortlandt, reaching a sealed letter towards the post rider, " do not I tell you that the malcontent captains were at the Council to-day, and that my father could not well place this in your despatches? — For, know you, it is a secret and confidential — "

" Hark, now," and Perry, the post-rider, still holding his horse's bridle, beckoned Gysbert and young Bayard across the path, so closely to the alder bushes where lurked the ambushed Abram that that young gentleman scarce dared to breathe for fear of discovery; "hark ye, young masters, know you not 'twere wiser to bridle your tongues so near to yon young scatter-brain ?" (And he nodded towards Barry Van Schaick.) " Secrets and confidences are not to be whispered so nearly to him. Why is he here?"

"Why, Perry," Gysbert explained, "'twas the only way I might get word to you when I missed you at the Lant-poort — by sending Barry across to Annekin Litschoe's to catch you ere you got to horse. And he knoweth nor suspicioneth naught of my message. See, Perry, here is a golden ducatoon for advance fee which my father, the Heer Mayor, doth send if you will but take the packet for him, and he bids me say that he will add to it two more such beauties if but you deliver it safe in Boston town."

"I may not well discommode the Worshipful Mayor," said the post-rider, as his hand closed on the tempting fee. "But his Worship, your father, must bear me out if aught of mischance cometh to me for this business, Master Gysbert. 'Tis a ticklish process doing aught for King James' sake these days, when — "

"Ho; pho!" broke in young Bayard contemptuously. "Be not so sure of that, John Perry. This affair of the Stadtholder is but a Dutch plot, my father sayeth, that cannot come to favor. And, in truth, I did hear my cousin Livingstone from

PERRY, THE POST-RIDER.

Beaverwyck,* say only yesterday that the whole thing was but a parcel of rebels gone out of Holland into England, and the Prince of Orange was at their head; but, good faith, he might never get out again, he said, but might, mayhap, come to the same end as Monmouth did."

"And that was—?" Gysbert said inquiringly.

Perry the post-rider drew his hand across his throat significantly, with a sharp "cluck" of his tongue, and then said, "Well, it might easily be so, young masters, but I bother myself with no such wonderments. I carry the post for the King's High Majesty, whosoever he may be, and I meddle not with changes. But—" and here he looked lovingly at the glittering fee and slipped the packet into his capacious pocket—"I will put this packet in my saddle-bags when I reach the Wedding Place† and see it safely through to Boston town."

What is it that pushes so stealthily out between the alder leaves and into the gaping pocket of Perry, the post-rider? It draws hastily back again,

* Albany.

† The "Wedding" place or "Wading" place, on the Harlem River near the old Boston post-road.

but it is not empty now, for with it comes the packet that but an instant before went into the post-rider's big pocket. Ah, John Perry, John Perry! you should not have pressed so closely to the alder bushes, for that gave the wary young watcher his chance, and the precious packet of the Worshipful Heer Mayor is now in the hands of Abram Gouverneur, the faithful young hench-man of the Heer Captain Leisler.

But Perry was all unconscious of this transfer, and leaping to his saddle, he cried out heartily: "Well, give you good day, young masters. My humble respects to your Worshipful fathers both, and "—this with a significant glance over his shoulder at the unconcerned Barry—"my grief that I may not lawfully act upon their request."

He was off like a flash along the heavily-shaded horse-path, and then Barry called lazily out: "And the stiver you promised me, Gysbert, if I brought John Perry to you?"

"'Tis all right, Barry; you shall have it as prom-ised," said Gysbert. "I'll get it from my father, and do you meet me at the Bridge by sundown.

Come now, Sommel.* I am for Walphat's Meadows † for crabs. And you, Barry, do you try for black-fish to-day?"

"Black-fish?" echoed Barry scornfully, as he lay, stretched at full length, beneath the chestnut trees; "do ye spy the size of those leaves, Gys Van Cortlandt, and then chatter about black-fish? Don't you mind Jan Airensen, the ferryman's rule?

> When chestnut-leaves are big as thumb-nail,
> Then bite black-fish without fail;
> But when chestnut-leaves are full a span,
> Then catch black-fish if you can.

See there; the leaves are full a span and more in bigness, and ne'er a black-fish may I take to-day."

He lay thus lazily till the two boys were fairly out of sight. Then his whole manner changed. "O ho, you smart ones!" he cried, springing to his feet and shaking his fist in their direction. "You thought to befool Barry Van Schaick with your packet and your pretences, did you? Hoy, lads;

---

* Samuel.

† The foot of Rooswelt street on the East River — now near the Bridge tower.

you need to rise betimes to get ahead of Barry Van Schaick! Quick, Teuny! run like the wind to big *baas* Ryckman at the mill. Tell him I say there's some blind game afoot — I know not what — between the grandees of the Council and they in Boston gaol. Say that a packet — not of the Council's — hath been taken secretly by Perry, the post-rider, to the Heer Governor Andros at Boston town. Speed now, and I will do the same to Captain Leisler or Captain Lodwyck at the fort."

But the packet was not on its way to Boston town, as Barry imagined; it rested safe in the pocket of young Abram Gouverneur, as he tramped across the Smits Vly to the Leisler farm; and silent and thoughtful while Mary chattered on, he wondered what it could be about, and, though sorely tempted to open it, said to himself, "'Tis unlawful to send a packet thus and therefore, sure, t'was right and fit that I should stay its passage. I will give it up to the Heer Leisler this afternoon when once I get back from the wolf-killing, and he may do with it as he deemeth best. There is,

sure, no haste needful, for Perry will never sus-
picion what may have come of it, even if he do
discover his loss before he makes the Wedding
Place. So — hey O, *belle* Marie," he exclaimed
aloud, " here be we at the *bouwerie* and there too is
Jacob, Jr., awaiting us. And he hath the goose-
gun all ready. Hurry!" and catching Mary's
hand he raced up to where Jacob, Jr., impatiently
beckoned for them. " Hollo, Jacob !" he cried.
" Here be we both ! And where is the wolf, and
how and when may we get at him ? "

CHAPTER VIII.

WHAT BECAME OF THE GOOSE-GUN?

THE Leisler *bouwerie*, or farm, was a large tract of open country, a good half-mile or so above the Land gate, covering the space now bounded by Printing House Square and the City Hall, Chatham, Vandewater and Spruce streets, one of the busiest sections of the mighty city nowadays, where all the news of all the world clicks and flashes each night into the offices of the great daily journals that line Newspaper Row from the Franklin statue to the granite home of the *Staats Zeitung*. Young Jacob, Jr., as the eldest son of the Heer Leisler was called, a handsome, lithe and well-built lad of seventeen, swung his arms in frantic welcome as Abram and Mary ran toward him.

"Well, where have you been all the morning?" he cried. "I am over-weary with waiting. But

O — he's a big fellow, I can tell you, Ab'm.   I have him safely housed in the bear trap yonder. They will surely add ten guilders seawant to our pelt-fee for trapping so monstrous a beast " — for so great were the ravages of the wolves among the sheep and cattle of Manhattan that the Council offered that year a prize, or pelt-fee of twenty guilders seawant* for the head of every wolf slaughtered and brought to the Stadt Huys by a "Christian," or half that sum if killed by an Indian.   "But come," said Jacob, Jr., catching Abram's arm excitedly, " come quickly and see him. And why did you come, Mary?   This, surely, is no place for girls."

"O, Jacob!" exclaimed his sister, drawing back in dismay, "the mother said I could come — and so, too, did Ab'm."

"Why, of course, Jacob — of course she can come," said Abram cheerily.   "Why, Marie is braver-hearted than half a score of such fellows as do run for their lives when that they see a bear flag fall."

* Twenty guilders in wampaum or Indian shell money amounted to about two dollars of our currency.

Jacob, Jr., yielded a brother's grudging assent and then, cautiously enough, the three drew near to the lodging of the imprisoned wolf.   Just about where now the hurrying crowds throng the New York approach of the great Brooklyn Bridge and almost beneath the Elevated Railway Station, stood the rough-hewn log bear-trap in which the gray wolf chafed and fretted.   A little dip, or valley, thick with low brush and alders, sloped downward to a stretch of swamp land, and the trap stood thirty yards or more from the sheepfold and cattle-pen, and, perhaps, two hundred yards, or more, from the quaint and low-roofed little farmhouse that stood, gable-end to the winding horse-path or country roadway, very near the spot where the *Sun* building now stands.

The stout logs of the trap creaked and trembled beneath the fierce attacks made upon them by the caged beast as he struggled for freedom.   The lads bade Mary perch herself in the branches of a wild cherry-tree near by while they clambered cautiously upon the roof of the trap and peered in upon their prisoner through the ample loopholes.

"Whew! but he is a monster fellow, Jacob," exclaimed Abram. "Ho-ho, Heer Bloody Jaws — do you not wish you might though?" And even he, brave as a young lion though he was, drew back with a start as, with a vicious snarl, the gray wolf sprang savagely at the darkened loop-hole and the voice. "How will we get at him, Jacob?"

Jacob, Jr., half-kneeling upon the roof logs of the trap, pushed back his hat reflectively.

"I did think to jam the nose of the goose-gun through one of the loopholes here, and pepper him in that wise," he said; "but I doubt me if we may get a fair sight at the beast in that way. What think you?"

"*Ma foi*, it is far too dark to sight any moveless thing through that hole, much less a rampant, roaring wolf," said the young Huguenot, thrusting a long stick through one of the openings to try for a "straight aim." With an angry yelp the wolf sprung at the stick and snapped it in pieces. "Ah, see there now," exclaimed Abram, "he hath an iron jaw though, hath he not? But — hoy — I have it, Jacob. Why could we not pry up the logs in front there just far enough asunder to let the old rascal's head slip through and then — pop! — we drop a running noose over him — you know I am good at that — carry the rope fast around that tree-trunk yonder " —

"Where Mary is?" interrupted Jacob.

Abram nodded. "Where Marie is now but will not then be," he replied. "Then, see you not, we shall have him fast held by the rope at one end, and the trap-log at t'other, and then we can pepper away at his head with the goose-gun while he essays to tug at the rope and the log."

It was a regular boy's plan; as novel and fool-hardy as well could be. But what boy ever stopped to soberly reason out a plan that promised so much of sport and excitement.

"The very thing," exclaimed Jacob, Jr. "Let us to it at once; run you to the cattle-pen, Ab'm, and fetch the ox-rope, while I get the goose-gun ready for his excellency."

The clumsy goose-gun, well charged with shot and slug, stood against the sheepfold bars, and Jacob, Jr., catching it up looked carefully at pan

and flint and priming, and then rested it against
the trap while he turned to help Abram rig a
strong and safe noose in the long ox-rope. Mary,
from her perch in the cherry-tree, watched the pro-
ceedings with gathering interest. There never
were, she thought, two quite so brave and handy lads
in all the world as Abram and Jacob, Jr.; and
soon the slip-knot was prepared.

"Now get you down from the tree, Mary," said
Jacob to his sister. "And go you into the sheepfold yonder. We need to make the rope fast
around yon tree-trunk, and you, sure, do not wish
that old Bloody Jaws shall leap into the branches
and keep you company. See, the fold is open, and
you can peer out at us between the bars."

So Mary scrambled hastily down from her
cherry-tree and posted herself inside the sheepfold; and, while Abram from the roof of the trap
stood ready to drop the noose, Jacob, Jr., also from
the roof, strove to force the entrance logs apart
just enough to let his wolfship's head squeeze
through.

How often, boys and girls, do we reckon without our host, as the saying is! Abram's plan was a capital one from his point of view, and might have worked well enough on a fox, or a 'coon or even a clumsy bear; but a strong and sinewy gray wolf was a "host" that should not have been left out in the reckoning. The logs, yielding to Jacob, Jr.'s cautious efforts, were first loosened and then slightly raised, and, quick as a flash, the dark gray muzzle and red fangs of the big wolf pushed through the opening.

"Now, quickly, quickly, Ab'm!" cried excited Jacob; "the noose — the noose — drop it over his snout!"

Almost as excitedly Abram lowered the noose and as the wolf's head now came pressing through between the lifted logs, the slip-knot settled behind the pointed ears and circled the bristling neck. Abram tightened the knot with a sudden and steady jerk.

"Ah ha; I have you now, Heer Bloody Jaws, sure and fast," he cried joyfully.

But if it is true that where a boy's head can go, a boy's body is bound to follow, how much more is it true of a long, lank, powerful-bodied wolf! The gray head struggled through the aperture that Jacob now tried in vain to close. His big pry-stick wedged itself between the shifted logs and, work as he might, he could not withdraw it. A great push of the wolf's strong and wiry shoulders drove the logs still farther apart, and now his body is following his head. Abram, tugging at the rope, tries in vain to force him back.

"O, Jacob, Jacob!" he shouted; "he hath the better of me. Quick—the gun, the gun!"

Alas; alas! in his eagerness to get the opening in readiness, Jacob had forgotten to bring the goose-gun to the roof with him. He leaped to the ground.

"*Ach, donder!*" he cried, rushing frantically from one corner of the trap to the other. "It is not here. O, Ab'm, where is the gun?"

"I had it not," answered Abram, his face flushed and his muscles overstrained with his exertions as he tugged at the rope for dear life. "Quickly now, or the beast will escape me. Now, now, Jacob, fire! fire at him—do!"

Fire at him? Alas, how could he? The goose-gun had disappeared!

Abram in desperation sprang to the ground, hoping to get the ox-rope around the trunk of the cherry-tree before the wolf could free himself entirely from the trap. But it was too late. With a last desperate and mighty thrust the great brute cleared the opening and with long leaps headed for liberty, dragging after him the plucky Abram. Jacob, not finding the gun, sprang to help Abram at the rope, but, ere he reached it, Abram stumbled over a half-buried log and was thrown violently forward, and as he did so the rope slipped through his chafed and blistered hands. Jacob, Jr., hard at his heels, fell over his prostrate body and, as the two lads lay helplessly sprawling across the unlucky log, the wolf, freed from restraint and dragging the long ox-rope after him, made straight for the nearest place of shelter where he might stand at bay against his pursuers. And that place of shelter was—where do you think?—the open sheepfold behind whose bars crouched the trembling and all defenceless maiden, Mary Leisler.

CHAPTER IX.

THE YOUNG SAKEMACKER.

BOTH lads sprang to their feet at once and, all unarmed as they were, rushed to the relief of this Seventeenth Century Red Riding Hood. But another rescuer was before them. For, ere the wolf's gray muzzle had touched the sheepfold bars, a quick step, a practised eye and a steady hand had stopped his progress, as, with a swift and sudden jerk at the trailing ox-rope, Papaig, the Kicktawane, had thrown the gray wolf on his haunches. Then, with a hasty turn, the rope was drawn taut around one of the posts of the sheepfold, a keen-bladed knife flashed in the bright sunlight, and ere the snarling brute could crouch for the spring, a lithe form had leaped upon him and the wary-eyed Indian drove the blade into the great throat. They had lost their pelt-fee, but Mary's life was saved.

"The young Swannekens * are swift," said the Indian lad, "but not so swift as is *Ma-iht-sho* † here."

"And *Ma-iht-sho*," said Abram, grasping the Indian's hand, "is not so swift as is Papaig. Surely, the pitying clouds must have dropped you for our help, Sakemacker,‡ for you did come in the very nick of time — did he not, Jacob? But come, *belle* Marie, do not tremble so," and he led the still terrified girl to her brother, "all is over now. See, here be Jacob, Jr., and here be I, and here lieth old Heer Bloody Jaws as dead — as dead as Governor Stuyvesant; and here, best of all, is Papaig the Sakemacker's son from Aspetong, but for whom you might have been '*hoof kaas*' for Heer Bloody Jaws even as Joost Stoll did prophesy. 'Twas a brave stroke, was it not, Jacob?"

Young Jacob Leisler, in his turn, grasped the Indian's hand. "Sakemacker," he said, "the peltfee is yours and so are our thanks. And a narrow escape it was for Mary. Said I not, Ab'm, that

* The Indian name for the Dutch settlers of Manhattan.
† *Ma-iht-sho*, Mohegan for wolf.
‡ The Dutch for Sagamore or chief.

here was no fit place for girls like her? said I not
so, Ab'm?"

"*Ma foi!*" exclaimed the gallant young Huguenot, rubbing his left ear reflectively, "you were
like to be nearly right this gait, Jacob, had Papaig
not come in the good stead he did. But then,
too, there would have been no such chance of mischief had you but been ready with your goose-gun
when I had our gray friend here fast in the
noose."

"Sure-lee!" exclaimed Jacob, Jr., hastily. "My
goose-gun! where can it be?" And in an instant
he was searching the vicinity of the bear-trap for
that so sorely needed and missing fire-arm.

The young Indian, too, joined in the search and,
dropping quickly upon one knee, studied the ground
critically. Then, turning to Jacob, Jr., he said,
"My brother's goose-gun hath been carried off —
but by no one here."

"Carried off!" exclaimed Jacob and Abram almost in the same breath. "Why, when — where,
Papaig? — and by whom?"

"Papaig can read it here," the young sagamore

replied, as, skilled in all the signs and indications of wood-craft, he pointed at the bright green grass. "My brother's gun hath been taken away by a young Swanneken brave, tall and stout as is my brother himself; with one foot heavier than the other; with one finger hurt as from a burn or scald, and with the shining buckles on his shoes and knees."

Jacob and Abram looked at each other in astonishment.   Both knew the marauder perfectly from the young Indian's description: — Gysbert Van Cortlandt !

"Papaig, you are a witch; you are a *jebi!*"* said Jacob, Jr.

"The son of Katonah the great Sakemacker is no *jebi*," said the Indian soberly. "It needeth no *jebi* to read the language of the grass, my brother."

"Yes, but, Papaig, how could he take the goose-gun from under our very noses, and we not see him?" asked puzzled Abram.

"Why did not the young Swannekens see Papaig

Jebi — Indian for sorcerer or magician.

when he stood watching them from the sheepfold yonder?" the Indian lad asked. "My brothers had all they could do to see *Ma-iht-sho* here. And when one who is not my brother's *nitap* * cometh crawling through the grass, as did the young Swanneken who bore away the gun, it is not strange that none did see him. Hath not this *Jonkheer* an angry heart toward my brother?"

"Ay, that hath he, Sakemacker," said Mary solemnly. "Why, he hateth them both as — as freely as they do him."

"Papaig can read the truth of the maiden's words even here," said the young sagamore, pointing to the grass, "and thus would the *shaw-go-da-ya* † delight it."

"O, the rascal," exclaimed Jacob, Jr., now grown very angry. "Wait but till I may lay my hand upon him. It shall weigh a ton."

"And where did you come from, Papaig?" asked Abram.

"The wigwams of my father, Katonah the Sake-

---

* *Nitap* — Indian for "a very good friend."
† The coward.

macker, are under Aspetong* and Papaig would gladly take one more look at the castles of the Swannekens," the young Indian replied.

"And so you shall," said Jacob, Jr. "Come, haste we back to the town, and you with us, Sakemacker. My father shall himself give you the whole pelt-fee and not the Indian's half. For sure it is your due. Cut off the beast's head, Papaig, and let us bear it before us as a trophy, stuck on a triumph pole."

"O, no, Jacob," pleaded Mary, shrinking from further sight of the dead wolf. "I cannot bear to look upon it."

"So ho, Mistress Fearful Heart," her brother cried scornfully, "here beeth a brave girl to join in a wolf hunt! You must not start back from such trifles as a dead wolf's head, Mary. Good faith, father sayeth 'tis the best kind of a wolf, that."

"And truly, *belle* Marie," Abram put in, "you should be over glad to see your old enemy so harmless now. There is naught to fright you in sticking thus old Bloody Jaws' head on a triumph-

* A bold bluff just north of Bedford in Westchester County.

THE TROPHY OF THE GRAY WOLF'S HEAD.

pole. And, sure, we would make a hunter of you."

So Papaig cut off the gray wolf's head, and while he dragged the carcass behind the sheepfold where he could find it and take off the skin at his leisure, Abram and Jacob hoisted the head upon a long pole, after which, bearing this trophy before them in triumph, the four headed straight for the Land Gate on the Broad Way at the Wall,

But as they drew near to the Land Gate they found their further progress barred by a few of their natural enemies, the *Jonkheers* who, with some of their henchmen and toadies (boys with money or power always have such followers, you know) fronted them there and would not let them pass the gate until they had answered a string of questions as to how, when, where, and by whom the gray wolf had been killed. At last Jacob, Jr., losing all patience, said sturdily, "Hold off your chatter now, and let us pass. And if you do think yourselves to know as much about wolf-killing as you do boast yourselves, why, talk you less and go a-hunting if you dare. Why, one growl from such a fellow as Heer Bloody Jaws there, would send you all *ongebondenheiden** to your mother's apron strings. So stand clear, I tell you, and let us pass, for we are for the pelt-fee."

"Ho, we are, are we?" cried Sommel (or Samuel) Bayard, standing out from the throng of boys. "So, so, mün heer High and Mighty *Eenkoren*,† do you own the town? Who hath the most voice here, I ask ye — a scurvy merchant's brat such as you, or the son of a worshipful member of the Governor's Council? See that you bridle your tongue, Jacob, Jr., or it may go worse with you — you and your wolf's head, and your pagan *bloodaard*‡ there, who seeketh to skulk in through the gate under your cover when you well know he hath no right to put even his nose within the city gate."

There was no disputing this offensive remark for, as Jacob, Jr., did know, it was indeed the law in those troublesome times that "no Indians or suspected persons" might come into the town save by especial and official permit or pass. But Jacob,

---

* Old Dutch slang for what we now call "skedaddling" — running home in a riot of terror.

† Nothing but a potato bug.

‡ A coward, a sneak.

Jr., was in no mood to be dictated to by his pompous young cousin Bayard; and he was about to force his way through at all hazards when he saw coming across from the King's Farm, Sergeant Joost Stoll and some six or eight harquebusiers of the city train-band making straight for the Land Gate.

Mary, feeling out of place as the only girl in all that throng of angry lads, had already left the scene, hurrying homeward down the Wall Street into which Abram had introduced her by squeezing her through an unpatched break in the palisade. But he, boy-like, as soon as he had seen her safely on her homeward way, hurried back to join in the anticipated fracas, and he reached the spot just as Joost Stoll and his harquebusiers came clattering up to the Land Gate.

"Come, scatter ye, scatter ye, for a pack of lazy ne'er-do-wells!" cried the sergeant of the train-band, full of his importance as a leader of men. "There is danger enough a-foot in the town this night without these boy brawleries. The train-bands guard the gates and I will have no loafing 'round here, *Jonkheers* and councillors' sons though ye be. You, Myndert, Jan, and Content Titus," he added, counting off three of the harquebusiers, "will keep your ward here at the Lant Poort, and let no sus- picioned person pass the gate unquestioned. You lads," he said to Jacob and Abram, "come with me to the Heer Leisler; he hath need of you. And — hollo! — what doth this Indian here? Doth he not know — why, so; 'tis Papaig, the young Sakemacker — and with the gray wolf's head. So, so, Ab'm; is that your *bouwerie* beast? *Sacara- mund*, but he is a monster one! Well then, come you in for your pelt-fee, Sakemacker; but, once in, you will not get out this night, for my orders from the captains are to let none pass the gates when once the guard is set."

But the young Indian loved his freedom too well to submit to this enforced visit.

"The son of Katonah will be no prisoner in the palisadoes of the Swannekens," he said. "Take you *Ma-iht-sho's* head, my brother," he added, turning to Jacob, Jr., "and when you do get the pelt-fee keep it for me or, better, bring it before the moon is old to Katonah's wigwams under Aspetong, and the young braves of the Rippowams and of the Kicktawanes will give ready welcome to Papaig's white brothers — both."

And, waving his hand in adieu to Jacob and Abram, the young Sakemacker strode off up the Broad Way, while the throng of lads at the Gate, with a chorus of defiance at Joost Stoll, turned their faces toward the town. But Abram and Jacob, still bearing their trophy of the gray wolf's head, followed Joost Stoll to the Water Gate where he detailed three other harquebusiers as night-watch at that point and then hastened down the Strand to the Stadt Huys.

CHAPTER X.

IN THE GOVERNOR'S CHAMBER.

THE two boys noticed the moment they drew near that all around the gray Stadt Huys swayed and surged an excited crowd. It was evident that they must have been drawn thither by some news or by some apprehension of trouble. They hastened, and as Jacob, still hugging his wolf's head, pressed in after Joost Stoll to claim his pelt-fee from the *voorleser*, or clerk of the council, Abram felt his arm clutched sharply and, looking around, he saw his volatile young friend, Barry Van Schaick, eager of eye and flushed of face, as if he had great news in store.

" Hoy, Ab'm ! " cried that excited young scrapegrace ; " here be rare goings-on. Folk say that the old Governor* hath his brigantine at Paulus Hook †

* Ex-Gov. Dongan, a former Royal Governor of New York.
† Jersey City.

full of Papists; and Teuney Fever-foot did see Gysbert Van Cortlandt and some of the *Jonkheers* putting off from the Copake rocks* on Luykus Bleecker's ketch and — O, why yes! Ab'm, now I do bethink me, he had Jacob, Jr.'s, goose-gun with him; how got he that?"

Jacob's goose-gun! Abram exclaimed in surprise at this unlooked-for proof of the correctness of Papaig's "grass-reading," but the glib-tongued Barry was too anxious to tell his story to wait for explanations.

"Yes, Jacob's goose-gun," he went on, "and they told Teuney they were off for the Navesincke to shoot sea-hogs,† but big Dirck Ryckman sayeth he knoweth they were set for Paulus Hook with word for the old Governor. And Tom Allerton saith that Jan Cruger and Mat Clarkson, who were sent as watch for strange sail at the *Conijnen*,‡ did spy two such bearing in for the Hoofden,§ and folk do say they must sure be full of the French

* Now Castle Garden.
† Porpoises — then as now very plentiful in the lower bay.
‡ *Conijnen Eylant* — Coney Island.
§ The Narrows.

king's frog-eaters. And Perry, the post-rider, is off two hours ahead of time with his despatches " —

" O — whew ! " And Abram gave such a long whistle that even Barry stopped in his recital. For he had just remembered his affair of the morning and the suspicious packet in his pocket. But Barry thought the whistle was for surprise at his news and he rattled on.

" Yes ; and all the captains are with the Governor and the Council ; and they have been having high and hot words. And I do believe me, A'bm, we are like to have the rarest kind of a row."

Barry had hardly caught his breath after all this long and hurried communication of his store of gossip, when his wary eye noted a movement around the entrance to the Stadt Huys, and he commenced afresh.

" Hey, hoy, Ab'm," he cried, " see, they are clearing a way. Here cometh the Heer Governor with the Council, and the captains. He looketh rarely vexed, doth he not — and the Heer Van Cortlandt too. Come along, let us crowd in and

ON THE STRAND NEAR THE STADT HUYS.

see them all.   Houf now, who be ye pushing, Claes Becker?   I have as good a right to see as you," and Barry, who was a regular weasel for pushing and wriggling into small places, worked his way through the crowd, followed by Abram, until they came very nearly to the open doorway through which the Honorable Mr. Nicholson, the English Lieutenant-Governor, was leaving the Stadt Huys after a particularly excited meeting with his Council and the captains of the city train-bands.

As the officials, some grand in their soldierly costumes, some sombre in their plain merchant's dress, came out into the Strand, Barry, prompted by a boy's ready spirit of mischief, raised a shrill shout of " Huzzoy for King William and Queen Mary!" and then dodged from view.   The Governor looked angrily around, and so did Col. Bayard ; and the latter catching sight of Abram exclaimed, " Ha ! 'twas Leisler's Huguenot cub."

And the Governor said, though his voice was almost lost in the cheer for King William that followed Barry's shout, " 'Tis a noisy rabble.   What do they here?   Col. Bayard, since your most valiant train-bands have seen fit to displace the soldiers of the King, it would, it seemeth, be wise for them to look to the dispersal of these riotous crowds."

Then, turning to the shouting throng, he said, "Good friends, 'twere better to curb your eagerness for the Prince of Orange until such time as ye do know whether he — "

But a still louder shout cut short his words: "Huzzoy for King William and Queen Mary!" "Long live the Stadtholder King!" and as the shouts, echoing from man to man, ran through the gathering crowd, the Governor turned sullenly away and hurried to the fort.

"So, young swaggerer," said Col. Bayard, as soon after he came face to face with Abram on the Bridge, "'twas you who would fain raise a riot around the Governor, was it? But that I have better work to do I would hale you to the cage or to the gaol."

"You are wrong, Heer Colonel," said Abram manfully, "I had no part in raising that shout. But I did join in it right lustily and so would I again, did occasion serve." And, dodging the quick pass of the choleric colonel's cane, Abram "made himself scarce" with marvellous celerity.

Two hours later, when he had slipped, unnoticed, into the fort on the search for Jacob's missing goose-gun which he heard had been given by Gysbert Van Cortlandt to one of the men in Captain De Peyster's company, he found a "row" in progress that would have done young Barry Van Schaick's heart good, and which accounted for his unchallenged entrance. For now the city trainbands had, on the demand of the captains, been detailed as reinforcements to the King's soldiers in the fort lest some sudden attack by the "Papists" and the dreaded French invaders should find the fort unprepared for resistance. There is always rivalry or jealousy between the "militia" and the "regulars" and here was no exception. For on this especial night Hendrik Cuyler the Lieutenant of Captain De Peyster's company ordered one of his men to stand sentinel at the sally-port. To this Sergeant Thompson of the King's troops strongly objected, and vowed that no Dutch bunglehead and butter-fingers should relieve the sentries of the King's High Majesty except upon His Worship the Governor's express orders. Words ran high, and when the news reached the Governor's ears a hasty summons came for Lieutenant Cuyler to attend his Excellency at once in the Governor's Chamber.

The usually placid face of the honest and easy-going Dutch lieutenant grew troubled and anxious — not from fear, for Hendrik Cuyler was as brave as any man in all the train-bands of the town; but as he said: " How shall I fare with the Heer Governor who knoweth Dutch no better than do I English ? Here, Cose Van Riper, come you with me to help me out or, *ach !* no ! here is young Ab'm Gouverneur; he is apt and smooth with the English speech." And, clutching Abram by the arm, he said, "you will do bravely. Come you with me to the Governor's Chamber."

Now Abram had just found and claimed Jacob, Jr.'s, lost goose-gun; and not knowing for what reason he was thus pounced upon and hauled away, supposed it was because he had been found in the fort where he had no business.

"O Hendrik; let me go," he pleaded. "I will get out instanter and will never come into the fort again without permission."

"Let you go? No, no, Ab'm, that will I not. You are of too much value for that," said the worthy lieutenant; and, almost before Abram understood the matter, there he was, with a murderous-looking goose-gun thrown over his shoulder, awaiting admission at the door of the Governor's Chamber.

On the other side of the door the ruffled Nicholson was pacing the floor greatly angered over this interference of the train-bands. He turned angrily upon Cuyler as he entered the room, with Abram and the goose-gun close upon his heels.

"How dare you tamper with my men, or seek to interfere with the disposition of the King's soldiers?" he broke out in wrath. "Who commandeth in this fort, sirrah, you or I?"

The jolly-faced Cuyler wished to appear respectful, but he made but sorry work with his broken English.

"Vell, Heer Gof'ner," he said, sprawling out his

big hands apologetically, "it vos — vos — not I dot vos — eh— *schuldig. Ich vos niet schuldig* * — *ach !* — how you call it, Ab'm?"

"Not your fault," suggested Abram from the doorway.

"Yaas, dot vos it," said the relieved lieutenant, "dot vos yoost it, Heer Gof'ner. It vos mein — how you call him? — *Hofmeister een der Burger-waght* † — De Peyster — dot vos der — der — *een rechter* ‡ — der —" and he looked again at Abram for help.

"The one who gave you the orders," suggested Abram.

"Yaas, Heer Gof'ner," said Cuyler, shaking his head vigorously, "dot vos yoost it. If I — what you call it? — insult the — the — *hoofd wagt* § — why — *ich — ich — barmhartigheyd zocke* ¶ —"

"A plague on your outlandish Dutch," broke in the angry Governor, while the astonished lieu-tenant who supposed he was getting on bravely,

* I was not guilty.
† Captain in the citizen guard, or train-band.
‡ The judge.
§ The guard of the fort.
¶ I ask your pardon.

backed hastily away from his Excellency. "A plague on your captains and your stupid trainbands, and a murrain too, say I, on your rebel and riotous town! You give orders forsooth? Why— I had as lief see the town burnt as be commanded by such as you. And — here — you sir!" he burst out in fresh fury, evidently first noticing Abram and his big gun. "Gad zooks, sirrah! how dare you push your way into the Governor's Chamber with such murthering weapons as that? Would'st threaten me, your Governor? Would'st cage me, if you dared, like to poor Mr. Andros in Boston town? or — mayhap — shoot me down? No — not while I have voice and freedom left. Out — out — out I say!"

And snatching a pistol from the table he charged upon his supposed assassins in a mighty rage and drove them from the room. Abram, surprised and considerably exercised by this unexpected ending to his interview with the Governor, looked to Lieutenant Cuyler for information and explanation, but that worthy member of the city trainband, puffing and flushed from his hasty and highly unsoldierly retreat, ruffled in dignity and manhood and completely at a loss for words, clutched Abram by the arm as they paused for breath at the north bastion and, shaking his big fist in the direction of the Governor's Chamber said huskily, "*Ach, himmel!* but his Excellency is passing wrathful. What doth he mean — and what doth he say, good faith? He would burn the town? Ay, he did say that. Put it down — put it down in your clever head, Ab'm, The Heer Governor did say he would burn the town and he did speak most disrespectful of the city captains and the train-band. Well! Here beeth a rare to-do! Here be pretty news for the captains and the citizens. They shall hear of this. Good faith, so they shall! They shall hear — they shall hear — " and with these mutterings spluttered in broken Dutch which we will not try to reproduce, and nursing his wrath to keep it warm the big Lieutenant strode to the guardroom to report the indignity to the Heer Captain De Peyster, while Abram still dazed and puzzled at the whole affair, shouldered the goose-gun and hastened homeward.

CHAPTER XI.

BARRY'S BONANZA.

THE Worshipful Heer Van Cortlandt, by favor of the king and by appointment of the Lieutenant Governor, " Mayor of Our Loyal City of New York in America," sat in his big house by the Water Side* wofully perplexed. For the Worshipful Heer Mayor was in a dilemma. His friend and patron, the Heer Lieutenant Governor, still held out stoutly for King James. But the people were already shouting, " Long live King William and Queen Mary ! " The city was in a ferment. Even now strange rumors were abroad of high words between the Heer Governor and the city train-bands, and the men, so the tidings went, refused to acknowledge the Heer Bayard as Colonel unless he declared roundly for King William and

* At the present northeast corner of Broad and Pearl Streets.

his English Queen.   And there were even rumors of strange threats against the Worshipful Members of the Governor's Council and against certain of the " Papists " and grandees of the town.   So the Worshipful Heer Mayor sat full of debate and ill at ease when suddenly through the open doorway young Gysbert Van Cortlandt came with tidings.,

"O, father, father," he cried ; " here is rare news !   Folk say that Ab'm Gouverneur did face the Heer Governor in his Excellency's very chamber last night and did seek to shoot him with his big goose-gun, and that the Heer Governor did chase him from the room with drawn sword and would have struck him down but for big Hendrik Cuyler of Captain De Peyster's company.   Yes ! and all the Dock Ward and all the South Ward are swarming around the Stadt Huys and the fort — and the Heer Bayard bade me summon you to a special council ; and — may I not have your fusil-lock, father ? "

"Nay, that you may not," replied his father. "But how say you — a special council ?   How then "—

But Gysbert broke in breathlessly upon his questioning. "Ah, but do let me have the fusil-lock," he pleaded. "For sure there will be need of it. 'Tis said Papaig, the Sakemacker, was seen with Ab'm by the Lant Poort yester night and folk do report, too, that all Katonah's tribe are to come to the help of the Stadtholder's people, So pray, father, let me have the fusil-lock. For I do much fear me lest Ab'm Gouverneur " —

" Always that young ribald ! " cried the Worshipful Heer Mayor. " Must he be ever mixed up with the city's brawl and babble ? The council and the captains must look to his chastisement. Things surely are sorely amiss when boys may brag and bluster on our very streets. No, sirrah ; you shall not have my fusil-lock. You would surely come to harm. Peace now," with a wave of his hand as young Gysbert's pout heralded fresh pleadings ; " no words, boy; I must even to the council straight," and, snatching from the settle in the broad hallway his cocked hat and stout cane, he strode importantly to the Stadt Huys where had gathered the Governor's Council for instant session.

And the headstrong Gysbert Van Cortlandt walk-ing straight to the great chimney-piece, whose pic-tured tiles told in inartistic groupings the chief of the Bible stories, and took down therefrom, notwith-standing his father's refusal, the polished fusil-lock.

For there were strange happenings in that little city by the sea on that most woful and exciting of Saturdays, the first of June, 1689. The affair in the Governor's Chamber had already been noised abroad. Tales grow more tortuous with each re-telling and here was no exception. Abram Gouver-neur, it was said, had braved the Heer Governor to his very face. Abram therefore was a hero. Not a boy in all the town but was proud of his acquaint-ance and envied him his fame. Even gruff Joost Stoll sounded his praises, and as for Barry Van Schaick — well, Abram, all excitement, had met Barry the night before on his way home from the fort and given him the whole story, and Barry, you may be sure, was not backward in making the most of the revelation, so that he was, I suspect, at the bottom of all the big stories that were now afloat and had largely helped at spreading the news. The

Heer Governor had sworn to burn the town and kill every Dutchman within the walls; the fort was to be taken and held for King James, and all the train-bands and all the captains were to be tortured in its dungeons; a whole fleet of French ships was even now off the Hoofden, and old Governor Dougan was to be made Lord High Governor and Dictator. These were some of the milder rumors that filled the troubled town and the people in sore dismay wondered what was to come next — of course expecting the worst.

But all this fuss and fume, all this trouble and turmoil were meat-and-drink for Barry Van Schaick. It was for him what the boys nowadays call " a regular bonanza." His eager and restless young spirit yearned for excitement and here he had it. The bigger the stories he could tell, the wider open he could cause the honest burghers' eyes to stand, the greater his glory and gratification. As, hour by hour, the town grew more and more unsettled as rumor and counter-rumor flew from street to street Barry ranged from Stadt Huys to fort and from fort to Stadt Huys on the alert for news and sensation — pushing, peering, prying. Now he was clambering within earshot of the open windows of the Council Chamber in the Stadt Huys through which came the sound of heated discussion between the Heer Governor and his council and the captains ; now he was hanging on the skirts of the crowd within and around the fort where in sturdy and determined speech the Heer Leisler exhorted the train-bands and the citizens to stand firm for King William and the rights of the people ; or now, linking arms with Tom Allerton, little Jan Crueger and other kindred spirits, he was darting along the narrow streets brawling out in rollicking tune the senseless but popular rhyme just then ringing from the throats of English Protestants and with which, so the old record says, they "**sung a** deluded prince out of three kingdoms " :

> Ho, broder Teague, dost hear de decree
>   Lilli burlero, bullen a-la !
> Dat we shall have a new deputie,
>   Lilli burlero, bullen a-la !
> Lero, lero, lilli burlero ; lero, lero, bullen a-la ;
> Lero, lero, lilli burlero ; lero, lero, bullen a-la !

In the intervals of one of these ringing choruses Barry saw, as he dashed across the Bridge in the Heeren Graaft (or Broad street), Gysbert Van Cortlandt striding along with a shining fusil-lock flung over his shoulder.

"Hollo; hollo, Gysbert!" he shouted. "Where away? to shoot sea-hogs — or Papists mayhap?"

A boy at the business-end of a gun is always invincible — in his own estimation. "I am like to shoot land-hogs — like you, Barry Van Schaick," Gysbert answered scornfully. "Look now," and he "covered" Barry with the fusil-lock, while that startled young gentleman dodged in sudden alarm.

"Have off, have off!" he cried. "You and guns are not over well acquainted."

Then, spry and swift as a monkey, he closed in upon the heavier and unwary Gysbert and, wresting the gun from his hands, rushed wildly down the Heeren Graaft while the astonished Gysbert followed close at his heels crying, "Stop thief! stop thief!" at the top of his lungs.

It so happened that, coming up the Heeren Graaft, was Sommel Bayard, the colonel's son, mightily important under his burden of a big drum which he had volunteered to bring from the fort for Sergeant Thompson's "regulars" at the Stadt Huys. Seeing the chase bearing in his direction, he laid aside the drum and heading Barry off held him fast until Gysbert came up. There was a struggle for the possession of the fusil-lock and then a sudden "bang!" as in the *mêlée* a blundering hand brought flint and lock together. Barry dropped the gun and darting at the drum, caught it up and in sheer excess of spirits began a loud rub-a-dub on the tight sheepskin. It was a simple and thoughtless boyish action but, simple and thoughtless as it was, it was as the spark to a train of powder. For as the crack of the fusil-lock and the roll of the drum fell upon the ears of the startled people they heard in them only the signal for the attack by the Governor's guards or the long expected French invaders.

"We are sold; we are betrayed; we are going to be murdered!" rose the mingling cries of alarm. Workmen dropped their tools; women rushed wildly to and fro and soon the whole city was in the streets.

"Hi, Ab'm, here is a rare to-do!" cried exultant Barry, catching his friend by the arm as he raced with the crowd to the fort.

"Rare, say you, Barry?" replied cooler-headed Abram. "It is liker to be more sorry than rare ere the night is on. Did you hear the gun and drum awhile back? Folk say 'twas the signal for old Heer Governor Dongan's brigantine to lead all the French ships straight to the town. The train-bands are in arms. Colonel Bayard will not head them; the Heer Governor is a Papist traitor and, faith, before to-morrow's sun it may be such another night here, for aught we know, as my mother telleth me her father, Heer Patem the captain, would oft tell her of — that awful day of St. Bartholomew."

Barry prudently kept silence as to the real story of the drum and gun and valiantly cried, "Who careth for the old Governor and his French ships? Are we not strong enough? I'll wager you we are. So, huzzoy for King William, say I, and hey for *Lilli burlero!*" and holding fast to Abram's arm he pushed through the crowd shouting the popular rhyme so boldly that many a voice caught it up and the streets echoed to the strains of the ringing chorus.

A boy's prank had started a riot that was fast growing into a revolution.   Around the fort the excitement grew higher and hotter.   Conflicting orders flew from Governor to train-bands and from company to company until none knew how to act.

"Off; I wash my hands of you all," the angry Colonel Bayard exclaimed as he turned his back upon the turmoil and passed out of the fort and through the excited throngs that filled the space within the fort and crowded the Merry-mount just outside the walls.

" Ho ; Bayard ! look to yourself ! " came back the angry shout mingled with jeers and hisses.   " You are a rank Papist and King James' lackey."

Some of the captains, seeking to stem the current of revolt, apologized for the rudeness of their men and begged the Heer Colonel to act as his commission warranted as Commandant of the Fort and the train-bands.   But even as they did so the determined cry went up :   " No Papists ; no Papists ! We want no dogs of traitors to be our leaders ! "

So swaying now this way and now that, the purposeless crowd, united only in their hatred of " Nicholson and his dogs " as they now termed the Heer Governor and his Worshipful Council, clamored and shouted, and Barry was in his glory. The tumult grew high and higher and no one seemed able to still it. And as he watched the leaderless confusion Abram said to Joost Stoll, who was flushed and panting from vain attempts to make himself heard, " ' Tis a pity, Joost, that the Heer Leisler were not here. For surely he is the only man fitted to still this tumult and counsel what to do."

" Ay, you are right, lad," said Joost. " He alone could do it. He alone could be trusted; for the Heer Leisler is the people's friend."

Abram's words had fallen on other willing ears. The word passed quickly from man to man: " Leisler; Leisler ! " rose the cry, and all knew it to be the name of a calm, clear-headed man. From group to group it ran, until as by a sudden impulse all faces turned towards the Strand and the conflicting voices all joined in the ringing cry which the people without the fort and on the Merry-mount caught up and rounded into the one tumultuous shout : "*Tot Leisler, tot Leisler, tot het huys von Leisler !*" (To Leisler, to Leisler, to the house of Captain Leisler !)

CHAPTER XII.

THE soft June airs brought fragrant odors of the early summer down the Strand from garden, orchard and clambering honeysuckle vine, and wafted cooling breezes from over the broad river and the Breucklen hills. But the fair Mistress Mary Leisler, though she felt the spell and promise of all the summer beauty, was not happy. For the bright young maiden was a lover of the open air and the freedom of field and hillside and all that rare June day she had been close prisoner within the house. Noise and strife filled the troubled city from the Fort to the Wall, and Mother Leisler had no mind to let her fair and restless young daughter mingle in the crush of the excited throngs or range like a hoyden beyond the compass of the motherly eyes. The long June twilight deepened into night. Now and then through the gathering darkness came sounds of uproar and of strife and Mary as she peered out through an open window tried to fathom their meaning and fell to wondering whether Jacob, Jr., was in it all and what Abram and Barry might be doing.

On the instant the sounds grew louder and nearer, they seemed coming toward her; soon lights were flashing along the echoing street and almost before her wonder had changed to anxious surprise the dim shadows took shape into approaching forms, and her sharp young eyes could discover by the light of the flickering torches the costumes and faces of staid burghers followed close by brawny-armed workingmen and restless, pressing lads. Still nearer they came and out of the clamor and uproar one word sounded distinctly in her ears: " Leisler ; Leisler ! " Her father's name.

They gathered before the door and filled the broad plaza in the Strand fronting the merchant's house. Had then the Heer Governor sent to apprehend her father, she thought, for the brave and daring words he had spoken to the people that very day at the fort? "Ah, I much fear me," she said half aloud, "that the Heer Governor and Colonel Bayard will seek his hurt. I will go down to him and warn him ere it be too late."

But before she could reach the foot of the broad staircase the shouts were redoubled in force and a thundering knock upon the outer door caused her to pause in alarm and, it must be confessed, to give a slight scream of girlish terror as it sounded so startlingly near to her at the foot of the long stairway. From the "dwelling room" came her grave-faced father, light in hand.

"O, father," cried his trembling daughter, "the Strand is full of clamorous men. I fear me that they mean your harm. Go not to the door, I pray you — or rather let me face them first. They would not harm a little maid like me."

"Nay, child," the father said, pausing even before he laid hand upon the latch to smooth the fair young head and look down reassuringly into the appealing eyes, "fear nothing for me. Your father hath naught to mistrust from any man in this town be he Heer Governor or chimney-boy. Go you to your mother while I open the door to our friends."

But curiosity, which was as strong in the maidens of 1689 as in those of 1885, stayed Mary's obedient footsteps ere she reached the door of the "dwelling room," as she heard the "lift of the latch" and felt the rush of the incoming evening air upon her flushed young face. She turned and looked toward her father. "What would you, friends?" she heard him ask as he lifted the light above his head to scan the waiting crowd. Its rays fell full upon the foremost faces, and Mary saw there certain grave citizens of the town whom she knew as friends of her father—the Heer Delanoy, the Heer Vermillye, the Heer Roelofse, the Heer Edsall — and close behind them the press and throng of a hastily gathered crowd.

"What would you, my friends?" the Heer Leisler asked again, and as he raised his hand for silence the noise and shouting ceased.

"Captain Leisler," said the Heer Pieter De La Noy, speaking for his associates, "much turmoil and strife filleth the town; none know how to act when the Heer Governor turneth Jacobite and

Papist and even our neighbors of the council cannot shape our ways. Need presseth to put this our government into the hands of some person of well approved fidelity and inclination to the noble Prince of Orange, and the citizens would therefore that you come to the aid of the town and by virtue of your office as captain of the train-bands and as a much respected burgher, cool of head and purpose, come even now to the Fort and take the command of affairs."

"Aye; Leisler, Leisler!" shouted the crowd anew.

" Nay, friends," came the voice of Mary's father as the tumult stilled, "it were wiser for you to choose some other than I, who have raised voice and word against the grandees and the Worshipful but unwise Counsellors of His Excellency the Heer Governor. It would, sure, scarce be seemly for so known an opponent as I to venture himself into the command, lest it should be said that I did seek to "—

But his words were cut short by the shouts of "Leisler, Leisler!" "You shall not say us nay!"

and from the rear of the throng came the steady tramp of armed men, and the gleam of the flickering torches fell upon the steel caps and corselets of the harquebusiers of the city train-bands — the free companies of the provincial militia. Their voices swelled the people's cry: "Leisler, Leisler! he shall lead us. Down with traitors and Papists! Huzzoy for Captain Leisler and the Prince of Orange!"

"Save the State, Heer Captain, ere the streets of the town do run with the blood of the people, shot down by the French and Jacobites," cried burly Joost Stoll from the head of his company, and as the shouts again filled the choked and thronging Strand, the Heer Leisler seeing that debate could be of no avail simply said, "Be it as you say then, friends," and withdrew to arm himself.

And as he did so Mary was sure she heard a sly rap at the kitchen door. So she cautiously opened its upper half and there, sure enough, she met the mischievous eyes of Barry Van Schaick and the excitement-flushed face of Abram Gouverneur.

"Dear faith, lads," cried the equally excited Mistress Mary, "how you did startle me! and what is it all about, pray ? " she asked, as Abram leaned in over the open half-door and the agile Barry vaulting easily up, perched himself upon it.

" 'Tis even as they say, *belle* Marie," said Abram; " the town is in a fury; the captains are undecided, the council are timid and are locked with the Heer Governor in the patroon's* house. The train-bands and the people say there is safety only if the Heer Leisler leadeth them. And so "—

"And so — and so," broke in the exultant Barry, " we are here, Mary. For we will seize the Fort this very night and turn out every Papist soldier and Jacobite traitor, and shout huzzoy for the Prince of Orange and for Heer Leisler, his loyal captain. Aye — and huzzoy for his pretty daughter Mary, too, eh, Ab'm ? "

"That will we for sure, Barry," chimed in the enthusiastic Abram. " For if, as folk do say there will be no rest until Captain Leisler be chief in command, think then what a great lady will you be, *belle* Marie ! May so low-born a worm as I hope for

---

* Frederick Phillipse, lord of the manor of Philipsebourgh or Yonkers, who had a town house near the Fort.

a word from so high-placed a lady as you will be ? "

" Have done with your chatter, you reckless lads,"
quoth Mistress Mary severely, yet evidently not dis-
pleased by the tenor of Abram's speech. " Have
done and get you gone ; for sure the mother would
say, did she know I held converse with you here,
that it was far from seemly for a maid to chatter
with such a pair of wander-foots. But O, Ab'm,"
she added as she pushed Barry from his perch and
then looked laughingly across the top of the half-
door, " O, Ab'm, did you find the goose-gun ? "

" Aye, surely did I, Marie," replied Abram, " and
faith I do think it was the cause of much of this
present turmoil ; " and then he told Mary the story
of the affair in the Governor's Chamber, and how,
too, he had passed the packet that he had taken
from Perry, the post-rider, to the Heer Leisler, who
had found it to contain matters of marvellous im-
port, for he had told both him and Jacob, Jr., to
watch well for Perry's return and acquaint him
therewith at once. Barry, to whom this tale was
now ancient history, slipped 'round to the Strand
to investigate the state of affairs, and soon the

closing of the outer door and the outburst of cheers told that the Heer Leisler had headed the determined train-bands, and warned Abram that if he would be " in the fun " he must cut his story short.

The news of the next morning was indeed startling. For the captains, forced on by the people and the train-bands, compelled the Lieutenant Governor Nicholson to deliver to them the keys of the Fort, and though the beleaguered Governor hurriedly summoned his Council and sought to stay the tide of revolt and maintain his fast-vanishing authority, he strove to no purpose. And so it came to pass that with this entry on the records of the Council, the administration of the Heer Lieutenant-Governor Nicholson came to an end:

The inhabitants of New Yorke ryseing this afternoon (6° day of June A° 1689) have taken possession of the Fortt, disarmed the souldiers and came with a squadron armed in Courtt, demanding the keys of the garrison and with force would and will have them.

And in the little Fort the soldiers and citizens signed a firm agreement to hold the city and the Fort, despite the efforts of the Governor, for the

" present Protestant power in England," while not many days after a Committee of Safety formed a temporary government at the head of which as " Captain of the Fort and Citadel " they elected " the loyal and noble Heer Jacob Leisler, merchant of the Winckel Street," as Commander-in-Chief, "until orders shall come from their majesties, and to do such acts as are requisite for the good of the province."

" All of which meaneth," said Jacob, Jr., as the young people gathered in council under the apple trees in the Dominie's Bouwerie, "that our father is the head of all and we are of far more import- ance now than Gysbert Van Cortlandt or Sommel Bayard, *Jonkheers* and grandees though they be."

" Wherefore, Ab'm and Barry," added Mary gayly, " you will please respect me as you ought and not demean my station by aught of the tricks that you were wont to play upon a simple mer- chant's daughter — but who is now — what is it, Jacob? a high-placed lady and daughter of His Excellency the Captain of the Fort and Citadel."

And the lads made humble obeisance before

UNDER THE APPLE TREES IN THE DOMINIE'S BOUWERIE.

the little maid and hailed her as the Lady Mary, Governess of the Province of New York, for the King's High Majesty and the Queen's Royal Grace.

Poor little lady ! Could she but have foreseen the sad and speedy ending of all this glory of a little brief authority she would have played the Lady Governess with less of sprightliness, and wished indeed that, for her dear father's sake, no such question as a conflict of kings and governors had ever come to plague and overturn the staid and quiet ways of that little Dutch city by the rivers and the sea amid those distracted days in Leisler's times.

CHAPTER XIII.

CAPTAIN MARY.

THE troubled days of the spring of 1689 passed as all troublous times must pass. The spring grew to summer and the summer to autumn. The blossoms of the peach and apple trees in the Dominie's Orchard hardened into fruit, and from Damen's Farm to the Smits Vly, and from the King's Gardens to the Wading Place the rich and glossy green of a beautiful summer made the island of the Manahadoes sweet with shade and verdure until the brilliant tints of an early autumn covered the dips and slopes with all the gold and crimson of the October woods.

But with the changing seasons there came but slight alteration in the exciting times that filled that little city by the sea with anxiety, and often with tumult. Rumors of faction and plot, and even of massacre, rarely founded on fact, but all the more dreaded when they proved thus unfounded, ran up and down the crooked streets of the town, and only the stout heart and strong hand of the People's Governor kept the very people themselves in check and thwarted the schemes of his enemies. Every man who seeks to benefit his fellows has enemies and often, alas, the more malignant as the man who excites their enmity is himself just and honest. And so it was with Governor Leisler. He had dared to stand out as the champion of the people, of their rights and of their religion; he had dared to accept in their name, and for their sake, a position of responsibility and importance; he had dared to defy that class in the colony which had heretofore held all the power, the wealth and the influence in New York, and for this he was feared and hated. He who accepts a trust, boys and girls, accepts grave responsibilities with it — an acknowledgment too often trifled with and overlooked in these present days of broken faith and tarnished honor. Well, care and responsibility made the governor still graver in face, still sterner in speech and manner, but he kept always a warm place in his heart, as he had always a ready and open ear for the voice, of Mistress Mary, his sweet young daughter, and the manly words of his boy protégé, Abram the Huguenot.

It was through the golden glory of one of the rare Indian summer days that the Lady Mary, as — half in sport, half in earnest — she was now called by her young companions, climbed the slope of the Verlettenberg and looked off toward the bridge and the wall to catch sight, if she could, of Abram or Barry who had promised to row her, together with Styntie and Tryntie Bogardus, across from the ferry stairs to the sandy beach that rippled and broke at the foot of the bold and cedar-crowned heights of Breuckelen, which the Indians called by the musical name of Ihpetonga and the colonists knew as *Remsen's Hoodgts.**

Now Styntie and Tryntie Bogardus were as comical a pair of trimly-built little Dutch lassies as could be found from the Hoofden to the Katz-

* Now Brooklyn Heights.

bergs. Their tightly braided hair fell in two stiff plaits on their broad linsey-woolsey shoulders, and their smile was as ample and as restless as their sturdy little legs. Barry found them great fun and so, too, it must be confessed, did Abram and Mary, even though it was a trifle beyond the dignity of a governor's daughter and a governor's clerk — for, to that position had Abram now attained — to trifle with such little girls overmuch. Soon, across the common that stretched toward the Land Gate Mary saw the fat little twins trotting along by Barry's side, and at almost the same instant she felt Abram's touch on her arm and heard his voice saying joyfully, " All is well, *belle* Marie. Mother Leisler hath given me a store of goodies for our eating; yon cometh Barry and the twins and my boat waiteth for us by the ferry stairs."

Away they raced to the waterside, and Barry and Abram were soon pulling across to the Breuckelen beach. Barry, of course, had a big story to tell for the wonder and perplexity of Styntie and Tryntie, of how Jan Jansen, a sailor on the Heer

Governor's brigantine, had sworn that he had seen a marvellous sea monster swimming off the " reach " by Nutten's Island, and how he, Barry, thought he could even then spy something that seemed like the monster's head bobbing above the water yonder, but how it might, perchance, be only a floating cask — and yet it might even be the monster.

"O Barry, is it so?" cried the twins in pleading chorus. "And what think ye — is it like to eat us up?"

"Why not; who else?" said Barry the incorrigible. " I am too tough; and, sure, no sea monster who knew his manners would presume to devour the Lady Mary, or the Heer Governor's *Geheimschryver* * here, so what can he do but take first Styntie and then Tryntie — or no, perchance it might be Tryntie first and then Styntie —faith I cannot say which."

"O, Barry, do have done," laughed Mary in spite of herself as the terrified twins looked to her for protection, turning from Barry in open-mouthed fear, their very braids quivering with

* Clerk or Secretary.

fright. "Have done, Barry, and tell us rather what came to you by the Lant Poort yesterday. For Ab'm did bring us rumor of sundry hard knocks between you and certain of the Jonkheers."

Barry rested on his oars and graciously allowed Abram to do most of the pulling across the dancing East River while he recalled the incident.

"Good faith, Lady Mary," he said ; " 'twas little save a brief show of might for us as why should we not now that we do have the stronger hand?"

"But my father sayeth that we are not to incense or affront the Jonkheers, doth he not, Ab'm?" said Mary with a certain show of reflected authority, as befitted the governor's daughter.

"Ay, that he doth," replied Abram, "and he sayeth well too; for, see you not, Barry, 'tis better for those who have the power to use it for the winning of their adversaries and not for brawls and warring. Now, I'll warrant me " —

"Nay, then, thou'll warrant me nothing," broke in hard-headed Barry. "But hear now, Ab'm — I'll warrant me that if Gys Van Cortlandt did but brave you with sore and biting words, you would fetch him a rousing cuff across his pate and serve him rightly too. I'll warrant me that if he did but say you nay, you would make it yea, or know the why thereof. Now Gys did say to me, did he, 'Oho; a fine commander is Sir Dog-Driver'—meaning your good father, Lady Mary—'that he doth let the fort and the palisadoes stay in such sorry posture after all his fine gloryings of what he would do. Pah!'—did Gys say, did he—'a very musk-cat could take the town now, and the munseers will have but easy work when they come to storm and sack.' And, good faith, Ab'm, as I did know it was even so but would not let him know I knew it, what, pray, could I do but answer him with a clip—as I did?" And Barry, quite breathless from his self-vindication, looked at Abram inquiringly and resumed his oars.

"But why may not the walls be put in safer guise?" asked Mary.

"Surely then, for lack of hands," replied Abram. "The Heer Governor, your good father, hath all that he may do to keep the town quiet and abate the factious diligence of the grandees

and keep the fort well-manned. There are none
to help upon the work."

"None, say you?" young Mary cried. "O, why
doth he not bid us all to work? Even us? Why
may not the children"—

"Hoi—ho!" Barry exclaimed, so sharply and
with such a start as to almost careen the boat and

OVER THE FERRY TO BREUCKELEN HEIGHTS.

to cause a double scream from both the frightened
twins. "'Tis the very idea, Mary! Why may we
not? Let us take a hand, rally the children in
the town and set them all to work lugging stones
for the repairing of the fort and the palisadoes.
Thus could we soon put it in excellent shape and
have some rare sport withal."

The plan struck both Abram and Mary as a

novel one and, indeed, so full of the idea did these
three young people become that, like all other
young people ever since the world was, they found
in the anticipation of untried employment more
delight than in the actual realization of their trip
to the Breuckelen Heights and considerably short-
ened that pleasant outing.   Much to the disgust
of those chubby twins, Styntie and Tryntie, they
hurried through their luncheon, curtailed their
climb to the cedar heights and rowed quickly back
again to the Water Gate.

The Heer Leisler listened to the children's proposal gravely enough, but a look of mingled surprise and pleasure stole over his face as Mary
unfolded the plan.

"'Tis well bethought, my daughter," he said,
laying a hand tenderly on her fair young head,
"and though it be scarce seemly work for maids
like you 'tis well worthy the desiring of such
earnest young patriots as yourself and Abram
here"—

"Ay, but, my father, 'twas chiefly Barry's plan,"
interrupted Mary, and that young gentleman with

a wave of his hand, part expostulation, part modesty, said virtuously, " Nay, trust me, Heer Commander, 'twas Mary's too, as well. It did but come into my head on her advisement."

" Well then, 'twas worthy all of you and cometh in goodly time and stead," said Heer Leisler, pleasantly. " For know, my children," he added gravely, " as indeed you are old enough to see for yourselves — there is still that stiff-neckedness among the grandees of this our troubled town to seek to discourage the people in helping me to haste on the fortifications, saying that it is but my notion to do so for my own glorifying. But trust me I will show them how by the aid of even such weak vessels as our children, the Lord doth achieve mighty things for his servants and doth get for us the victory. Gather the children together then, I pray you, and by to-morrow's sun we will get to the completion of the walls."

And beckoning Abram to follow him, the Heer Leisler walked quickly towards the Stadt Huys while Barry as Mary's lieutenant in the enterprise — " Captain Mary " as he now called her —

sped through the town summoning the children for the morrow.

"Captain Mary's" forces were early in the field next day — a quaint and curious host of helpers in linsey-woolsey and in homespun stuffs, clumsily cut, and still more clumsily made according to our modern tastes. But no Nineteenth Century boys and girls in knickerbockers and jerseys ever enjoyed their play more thoroughly than did this crowd of youngsters of two centuries back as they tugged and lugged and fetched and carried, working like little beavers but with all the zest of play. "Since two dayes agoe," writes the Heer Leisler in one of his carelessly spelled letters to the Worshipful Governor Treat of the Connecticut colony, "the children have worked and have gathered in one daye above an hundred lode of stonnes." You boys and girls who have played at building docks or helped at laying walls know that this was no easy job. But "Captain Mary" was a cheery young guiding spirit, and Master Barry was a most efficient "baas" or director. The workmen soon had at hand all the needed material to patch up the broken walls and the ruined palisades, and the town was again well protected, thanks to the pluck of the children.

And when the last stone in the defences was laid, and the red flag of England floated above the walls of Fort William in honor of the event, Abram, like a loyal young supporter of the newly-acknowledged sovereigns of England, sprang on a pile of stones near to the north gateway of the fort, and, swinging his hat called out lustily, "Huzzoy for King William and Queen Mary!" which being given with a will, Barry from the same vantage-ground shouted out with the full force of his strong young lungs, "And huzzoy too, say I, for Captain Mary!"

The cheers rose with a mighty will alike from harquebusiers and volunteer workmen, from staid old burghers and from all the boys and girls, while Mistress Mary blushed furiously and knew not which way to look in her confusion. And as the cheers died away the three young people standing by the gateway of the fort heard a deep voice say "Amen to that! This maiden is my brave little daughter, friend Jacob, whom you have scarce seen since she was a babe, and by her devices have I been able to put the fort in good posture as I have even told you."

"A brave maiden and a comely one," Mary heard a second voice reply and glancing up she saw standing by her father's side a tall dark man of thirty-five or thereabouts, sombre alike in dress and face from his steeple-crown hat to his broad buckled shoes, who regarded her with so steadfast and searching a look that she flushed deeply beneath his gaze and looked to the ground again.

"Who may he be, Ab'm?" she asked, in a hurried whisper as soon as opportunity served; and Abram as hurriedly replied, "'Tis your father's good friend, the Heer Jacob Milborne, *belle* Marie, just from Holland in Dirck Wessells' brigantine the 'Great King Solomon.'"

CHAPTER XIV.

THE BOY SECRETARY.

THE office of *Geheimschryver*, or clerk, to the Heer Governor, which dignity, as intimated in the preceding chapter, young Abram Gouverneur had now attained, had been given him because, as we learn from the records, he had a remarkable education for so young a lad and because he could readily read, write and speak the three languages chiefly spoken in New York — that is to say English, Dutch, and French.

And thus did he repay his mother's care for him in the old home across the seas as well as the Heer Leisler's doings for his welfare in the new world.

And in the rich autumn days, in the fall of 1689, the people of the island city, at the request of their now popularly constituted Governor, met and

for the first time in the history of the city, if not of
America, elected by their own voice as Mayor the
Heer Delanoy — that honest burgher who had
headed the deputation which, that turbulent night
on the Strand, had requested the Heer Leisler to
take command of the fort. Mayors the city had
known for many years, but they had been the ap-
pointees of the Royal Governors and held office
only at the pleasure of their patron and superior.
But the Heer Delanoy was regularly elected by
the representatives of the people themselves, and
at the suggestion of the Heer Leisler who, therefore, stands recorded as the first American who
appreciated and acted upon the idea of personal
liberty and personal choice which has so helped to
make America the land of freedom and of free-
men. And at the same election the wisdom of
the Governor was further justified by the election
by the people of young Abram Gouverneur as
clerk of the town — a rare instance in history of a
civil office going by election to so young a man.
And in the old records we find this note of the
fact:

Whereas: By order of ye Committee of Safety it was ordered, that ye Mayor Sherife and clerk shall be chosen by
ye Mayor and votes of ye freeholders. Come to Peter De
La Noy, Esqr., for Mayor, and Johannes Johnson for Sherife and Abra. Gouverneur for clerk who were accordingly
confirmed as viz : By the Commander in Chief, *etc.*

That Abram fully appreciated the honor and felt
the responsibility that rested upon him, we have
the judgment of his associates to prove as we find
it recorded that he "kept the records with great
clearness and precision." And at the same time
he felt, as do most conscientious boys who have
been placed in responsible positions, that whatever was in the interests of the colony was in
his path of duty. He therefore kept a sharp eye
upon all the doings of the day in and about the
town, alike among the friends and the enemies of
the new order of things. It must here be confessed
that Abram did not take kindly to the Heer Jacob
Milborne, whom the Governor had appointed as
Secretary of the Province and Clerk of the Council. He could not have told you why. It was
much the Latin epigram of Martial over again :

Non amo te, Sabidi, nec possum dicere quare;
Hoc tantum possum dicere, non amo te.

Translate it, you boys and girls who are rising Latin scholars; or, if you cannot, here is the way old Tom Brown, at just about the date of our story, translated it so as to apply to a man he did not like, Bishop Fell of Oxford:

I do not love thee, Doctor Fell,
The reason why I cannot tell;
But this alone I know full well,
I do not love thee, Doctor Fell.

Which was Abram's case exactly. Although, as Barry, who was of the same way of thinking, expressed it, " And how could you, Ab'm? Why, there's more laugh in one wrinkle of old Patem Byvanck, the inviter to funerals, than there is in all Heer Milborne's corpus. A man whose face is as dark as is a thunder-wrack over Corlear's Hook yonder is no merrier comrade withal than was the Heer Bloody Jaws that you and Jacob, Jr., trapped at the Leisler bouwerie." But this was no tangible reason; and though Abram and the Heer Milborne had but little friendly talk, the young clerk sought to so act as not to make him an enemy. For he knew him to be the Heer Leisler's friend and, though a stern, yet a shrewd and practical adviser withal at a time when such friends and advisers were sorely needed in the colony.

But if friends were needed enemies were in abundance. And none more bitter than those who before had been high in power and impor- tance. The Heer Van Cortlandt and Colonel Bayard were, by far, the most active in their hatred and enmity towards the People's Commander. And though compelled by the will of the people to fly for their lives, they still carried on their plots from beyond the city walls and sought to work ill to the struggling colony. And, while fearful of conspiracy at home, the little city felt, too, all the dread of a suspected foreign invasion. For by every ship and by every post-rider, came fresh and stronger rumors of French designs against the troubled town. How that the Count Frontenac from the Canadian country was to lead a mighty armament against the poorly-defended town ; how

that first Albany and then the English towns of
the Connecticut colony were to be sacked and
destroyed; how that next the fort and town of
New York were to be given over to pillage and
plunder, the Huguenot refugees to be put to the
torture and to death, and "all the officers and
principal inhabitants from whom ransom could be
exacted to be detained in prison." Indian sav-
agery and all its attendant horrors of ambush and
massacre were to be brought upon the city and so,
fearful of false friends within and bitter foes without, the little Knickerbocker town lay in perpetual
ferment and continual fear.

It happened that one clear and crisp December
day as Abram and Barry tramped up to the doorway of Conradus Vanderbeck's half farmhouse,
half tavern, near the Kolch, to borrow an axe with
which to cut a hole in the ice on the Fresh Water
for winter fishing, they spied a big bay horse tied
to the bars of the hovel just back of the house.
Both lads stopped surprised.

"Perry's bay," exclaimed Barry.

"What doth he here, think you?" said puzzled

Abram ; for both the lads knew that Conradus Vanderbeck's house was altogether off the route of Perry, the post-rider, whose road lay straight from the Wading Place on the Harlem, past the Halfway House (now 109th street) and down the post-road to the Land Gate and the Stadt Huys. Ever since the affair of the packet — mentioned in an earlier chapter — which disclosed certain plans of the "aristocrats" and the Heer Governor Nicholson against the intent of Heer Leisler and the people, Abram had held grave suspicions as to the integrity of the dashing and popular post-rider. And to find him thus loitering off his route redoubled his misgivings.

"Hist, Barry," he said; "go softly and spy out the cause. Here is surely something awry, when the post-rider rides turns from his road."

Barry, born trapper and keen-eyed scout, dodged past the broad doorway and around the corner of the house and soon returned, weighty with tidings, to Abram secreted in the "cripple-bush," or brier thicket.

"'Tis Perry, true enough," he said in exultant

whisper, "and with him are Conradus Vanderbeck and Jan De Grauw and big Hendricks from the Bark Mill. And they are saying somewhat of a package from the King's Majesty to the Heer Commander which they seek to get for the grandees."

"So!" exclaimed Abram, excitedly, "here is treachery abroad. We must learn more, Barry. But how? Can we not raise the window—or stay—there stands the cellarway, unclosed; let us drop down and listen to their plans from the ladder that leadeth up to the tap room. We must reach the bottom of this matter, Barry, for it may be that much of importance doth depend."

No sooner said than done. Cautiously and carefully the two nimble young fellows drew close to the open cellarway and dropping into the dark vault groped their way through casks and blackness to the steep ladder that led to the floor above. Then, crouched on the upper rung and on the narrow doorsill, Abram and Barry "laid low," as the boys say and listened "with all their ears."

"There's no time to be lost," they heard Perry the post-rider say. "There is no doubt about the packet, for I myself had speech of Master Riggs the messenger in New Haven town, and saw the paper. It is from the King's Majesty himself and thus is it addressed: 'To our Lieutenant Governor and Commander-in-Chief of our Province of New York in America, and in his absence to such as for the time being take care for preserving the peace and administering the Laws in our said Province of New York in America.' You see I have all the words pat and proper, and it stands thereby that whoso getteth deliverance of the King's Packet first hath authority to take the power in this Province; see you not then that if the old Governor's Council shall get it first it will be for their behoof — and ours, if we shall get them news and sight of it? The Heer Van Cortlandt will pay royally for this chance for power. So, saddle your horse, Jan De Grauw; speed as for dear life straight to the lord patroon's at Yonckheers where are now the Heer Van Cortlandt and Colonel Bayard. Tell them of the King's packet and how I

will seek to get Master Riggs unseen into Colone
Bayard's house.   Quick, for — holo! what's that?"

Perry the post-rider turned with a paling cheek.

What was it indeed!   Alas! for too inquisitive
ears.   The ladder, not over well secured, had
slipped beneath Barry's eager movements and
fallen heavily to the ground with a resounding
crash while the two lads just saved themselves by
clinging to the narrow sill, kicking out wildly for
safety and a foothold, but both bravely repressing
any sound of astonishment or dismay.

"Quick, drop," whispered Abram, as the sound
of hurrying footsteps sounded on the floor above.

"All right," assented Barry. "Here goes. Make
for yon streak of light.   'Tis our only chance."

They dropped into the darkness and uncertainty
below them and without a word dashed across
the gloomy cellar at the imminent risk of cracked
heads and broken shins, fled wildly through the
open cellarway and only halted for breath when
in the security and briers of the thick "cripple
bush" behind the hovel they crouched, listening
and panting.

CHAPTER XV.

WHEW," panted Barry; and "whew," echoed Abram from the safe covert of the cripple-bush. "Sure, 'twas a narrow squeeze. D'ye think they can track us here, Barry?"

Barry peered anxiously through the thick brush. "They can but, faith, they will not. See, Ab'm," and he parted the brush for his comrade, "yon they go townward. They are off the scent." And then, swiftly but stealthily, the two lads hurried through the dense woodlands to the Broad Way and entered the town by the Land Gate, safe and sound.

"Barry," said Abram as they hurried on, "we must get news of that packet to the Heer Leisler or, better still, get speech and sight of Master Riggs himself before Perry and the grandees bag the game."

" Aye, that we must," admitted Barry, " but how, think you ? "

They discussed the matter as they hurried down the wall and it was finally agreed that Barry should hasten to the Stadt Huys or the fort to inform the Heer Milborne of the approach of Master Riggs with the King's packet while Abram himself, turning northward again, should watch the post road so as to intercept the messenger before the post-rider could do so and conduct him at once to the fort instead of to Colonel Bayard's house as was the plan of the conspirators. Abram therefore turned in his tracks and sped over the hills by short cuts to the Halfway House, and Barry, equally full of zeal, hastened in much excitement to the Stadt Huys. But, failing to find the Heer Millborne there, he would have searched for him at the fort had he not encountered Tom Allerton on the Strand and learned from him that a whale had been bewildered in the swirl of the *Hellsgat* eddies and driven ashore on Great Barent's Island (now Ward's Island). All recollection of his errand was driven clean out of his head by this new and startling piece of intelligence and, yielding easily to Tom's entreaties, he hurried with him to see the captive monster and then spent a good half-day lending a helping hand while Joris Dopsen, the fisherman, cut the fellow up. Abram, more intent on his mission, intercepted Master Riggs before he reached the Halfway House, took him townward by the Sapokanican * road, thus avoiding a meeting with Perry, the post-rider, and so brought him safely into the fort and the presence of the Heer Commander Leisler even before the "grandees" who were summoned to Colonel Bayard's house had heard of Master Riggs' arrival. But when they did hear of it and appreciated the full importance of the fact that the coveted packet from the king had reached — as indeed it should — the hands of their hated rival in power, the people's champion, their rage knew no bounds, and had plucky young Abram fallen in their way or in that of the baffled post-rider it would have gone ill with him.

As it was, they hastened to the fort and de-

* Sapokanican, afterward Greenwich village, now the crowded Ninth Ward of New York, south of 14th Street and Eighth Avenue.

manded that the packet be delivered to them because they had been the late king's councillors;
but the Heer Leisler denied their rights, declared
that the people had invested him with the authority
and that, as he was the person, as the packet stated,
who "took care for preserving the peace and administering the laws" in the Province, he was
the only one authorized to receive it.   He threat-
ened them with punishment if they dared disturb
the town by their claims and plottings, and after
many high and hot words had passed the baffled
"grandees" left the fort enraged and defeated.

"How happened it, Heer Milborne," demanded
the angry Colonel Bayard, suddenly encountering
the sombre-faced Puritan secretary on the bridge
in the Heeren Graaft; "how happened it that we
knew naught of the arrival of the king's messenger?"

"The king's messenger, say you; what messenger pray?" demanded Heer Milborne in some surprise, for, thanks to Barry's carelessness, he had
heard nothing of Master Riggs' arrival.

This angered Colonel Bayard still more, for he

felt that the friend of his enemy, the Heer Commander, was seeking to deceive him.

"No trifling with me, sir secretary," he said hotly. "Have you the assurance to assume that you know naught of this foul play of your master in the fort yonder? It shall go ill with you, sir, if you shall dare trifle with the king's authority!"

"Nay, sir," said the Heer Milborne haughtily. "Such threat doth not now lie in your power. But truly I know naught of this matter. Hath Master Riggs in truth arrived? I will even now to the Heer Governor at the fort and inquire what this meaneth for, truth to tell, it is most surprising — ugh, pouf, ugh, — what meaneth this, then!"

Nothing but Barry again. For, just as the Heer Milborne turned coldly away from the angry ex-councillor, down the Heeren Graaft and across the bridge dashed heedless Barry now thinking only of his forgotten message. Head down and with no eye on the outlook, he ran full against the upright person of the sombre Heer Milborne with so sudden a shock as to send him staggering against the equally unprepared colonel. It was a terrific collision, and for an instant it seemed as if the three victims of the surprise would go sprawling into the canal. But, thanks to the bridge-coping, they recovered their balance and, with an angry glare first at each other and then at the irrepressible Barry, both gentlemen broke out in heated exclamations.

"You graceless young varlet," began Colonel Bayard; and, "You misbehaving blunderhead," cried the Heer Milborne, "what meaneth this disrespectful headiness that doth nearly tumble your betters into the ditch?"

"O, Heer Milborne," exclaimed Barry, when he had regained his senses and his breath, "I have been searching everywhere for you. Master Riggs, the king's messenger, hath —" and then, remembering that Colonel Bayard was of the opposing party, he clutched the Heer Milborne's arm and, hurrying him off the bridge, gave him his belated message.

The Heer Jacob Milborne was very jealous of his position and authority, and Barry's carelessness sorely wounded his pride. He thrust him to one

BARRY IS CALLED TO ACCOUNT.

side exclaiming, " Foolish idler ; why was I not acquainted with this before !" and hastened to the fort, leaving both Colonel Bayard and Barry, equally unsettled, on the bridge. Not feeling entirely at ease in the choleric colonel's company, Barry judged discretion to be the better part of valor and took to his heels without delay, while the angry colonel, still fuming with rage, strode back to his house to confer with his associates.

The next morning Barry, full of remorse for his heedlessness and forgetfulness, sought Abram out to make a full confession and beg his forgiveness. He found him at last at the tanyard near the Madje Padje, which, since Joost Stall's departure to England with letters from Heer Leisler to the king, he had been obliged to occasionally visit and overlook for his patron. Abram readily forgave his contrite young friend, all the more freely because he had compassed his ends without him.

" But," said he, " the only regretful thing is, Barry, that the Heer Milborne plainly thinketh that we, both, did deliberately and incontinently keep him from being advised of the coming of the king's packet, to the intent that we may obtain all the more credit from the Heer Governor while he getteth none. I would, therefore, that you had found him out at the desired time, for, faith, the Heer Secretary doth misjudge me sadly in many things, and this in especial."

"Well, it was sorely stupid of me," admitted Barry. "But truly, Ab'm, now that it is over, I care but little for the Heer Milborne's concernment. It is well, say I, to take such as he down to ground once in a while. A Lord High-Cockalorum! Doth he think that you and I are but black Barbary negro-men and he the Soldan of Muscovy whom all must bow low to, forsooth! I am glad I did forget," and, quite heated in his safe defiance of the sombre Heer Milborne, Barry helped Abram in his work and before noon arrived both lads were hurrying back to see what might be the state of affairs in the fort. On the Strand they saw Jacob, Jr., running as if for dear life towards the Stadt Huys, flushed and panting.

"What's awry?" demanded Barry, halting the eager runner.

"Enough is awry; everything is awry," panted Jacob, Jr., grasping both his friends. "More danger is afoot. That firebrand of a Bayard with a rabble of his following are pouring down the South Ward to the fort, and I fear some mischance to my father from their hands, which being feared I am minded to call the citizens by sound of the Stadt Huys bell to succor him. So, hurry you both, and if there is aught to fear, speed Teuny Fever-foot or some swift messenger to me and trust me to set the bell a-ringing."

Down the Strand and quite to the edge of the Bayard crowd pressed the boys and then, slipping around to T'Marckvelt, reached it just in time to see the Heer Leisler pass out from the fort and cross the wide market space, now known as Bowling Green, in the direction of his home on the Strand. And Abram saw to his dismay that Mistress Mary was with her father. Out from the Brouwer Straat* surged the angry crowd and with threatening shouts bore down upon the calm-faced Governor, who stopped and stood his ground.

* Now Stone Street between Broad and Whitehall.

"So, sir," called out Colonel Bayard loudly, "you would fain be the King's Governor, would you? We shall see who be the masters here. Seize him, or cut him down!"

Abram sprang valiantly to the side of his patron and placing Mary behind him, thrust into the Heer Leisler's hands the pistol which he had fortunately taken with him to the tanyard to kill a thieving polecat. Barry catching sight of the little Indian lad Teuny Fever-foot on the outskirts of the crowd drew him quickly off and said hurriedly, "Run, Teuny, run as for your life to the Stadt Huys and say to Jacob, Jr., ' Ring — ring — ring!'"

Then as the fleet little Indian sped away Barry hurried to Abram's side and clutched a cudgel valiantly. The levelled pistol of the Heer Governor was an unlooked-for obstacle and the foremost of the mob hesitated.

" Heer Colonel," said the Governor gravely, " I have no fears from your threats. But this shall prove a serious matter for you, if you shall dare obstruct the duties of the King's Governor."

This was but as fuel to the flames.

"The King's Governor, say you?" cried the enraged ex-councillor. "Tyrant, blockhead, dog-driver, how dare you seek to play so high a part! Down with him, friends?" And as the swift, up-swerving sweep of his stout cane sent the pistol whizzing from the Heer Leisler's grasp, the crowd drew closer around the beleaguered Governor. Then as Barry, at Abram's quick suggestion, dragged Mary out of the press and darted with her across the Marketfield towards home and safety, and as Abram thrust his cudgel into the Governor's hand, and held a jagged stone in his own, suddenly upon the ears of the startled crowd sounded the loud and rapid clang of the Stadt Huys bell.

"Jacob, Jr., hath the word," said Abram to the Governor. Then he cried out, "Ho, goodmen and true! rescue, rescue for the Heer Governor! Rescue from traitors and Papist dogs!" A blow from a staff sent him staggering back, closer and closer pressed the crowd around his patron, hands were stretched out to grasp him while still above the din rang out quick and clear the sound of the alarm bell. The Heer Governor was in a tight place.

CHAPTER XVI

AT THE WEDDING PLACE.

DENSER grew the mob, hoarser and angrier rose the shouts around the beleaguered Governor. Young Abram Gouverneur picked himself, bruised and sore, from the ground only to go down again under the blow of a ready pike-staff. The Heer Governor was powerless — one against a host. Escape was impossible; capture or worse was imminent. But never for an instant showing the white feather, the Heer Lei er faced the angry mob alone.

"Cravens," he cried in stern and steady tones, "these be rare doings for a loyal city of King William! Touch me at your peril! For myself as Jacob Leisler, burgher of this town, I have no care or concern ; but as the lawful representative of his Gracious Majesty the King, such touch is heretic treason. Stand off now, and disperse ye to your homes, or, by the sacrament! he who dares to brave my word shall rot in yonder jail. Disperse ye then! disperse!"

The throng of malcontents quailed before this heavy threat, for they all knew that the Heer Jacob Leisler was a man of his word. But the hot-tempered Colonel Bayard was too headstrong to calmly consider the consequences.

"My head against his, friends!" he cried. "Who is there among ye that trembles at this Sir Dog-driver? I am higher in the colony than he. I am Colonel of His Majesty's loyal train-bands, and this Leisler, as ye know, is but a traitor captain in my following. In the name of the king, I charge ye lay hands on him and haul him straight to the goal so that this our goodly town may have ease and rest from his plottings."

"Bayard, thou art a scurvy knave," said the Heer Leisler, still holding himself at bay. "This is but sore return for the good office I did for you in this same strait, when that you were set upon by the citizens in the Winckel Street as ingrate and

Papist and naught but my word and pledge could save your useless life. I ask naught for myself, but as your Governor and the representative of your King I charge you, on your allegiance, give me passage!"

"Philistine and arch-rebel," began Bayard hotly —but what else he would have said or done history does not record, for just then around from the Heeren Graaft came the shout of rescue, and a crowd of townsfolk led on by the Heer Milborne and young Jacob, Jr., came hurrying to the spot. At the same instant Abram who had again found his feet dashed madly across to the fort shouting at the top of his lungs that the Governor was in peril. The drums beat to arms; the train bands poured out of the fort and charged to the rescue while the baffled mob of malcontents scattered hastily in all directions and the Heer Governor was safe.

But the Heer Leisler was a man of his word. As the acknowledged Royal Governor of the province he visited swift and merited punishment upon his bitter enemies whom he had hoped to conciliate but must now overawe. He issued warrants for the

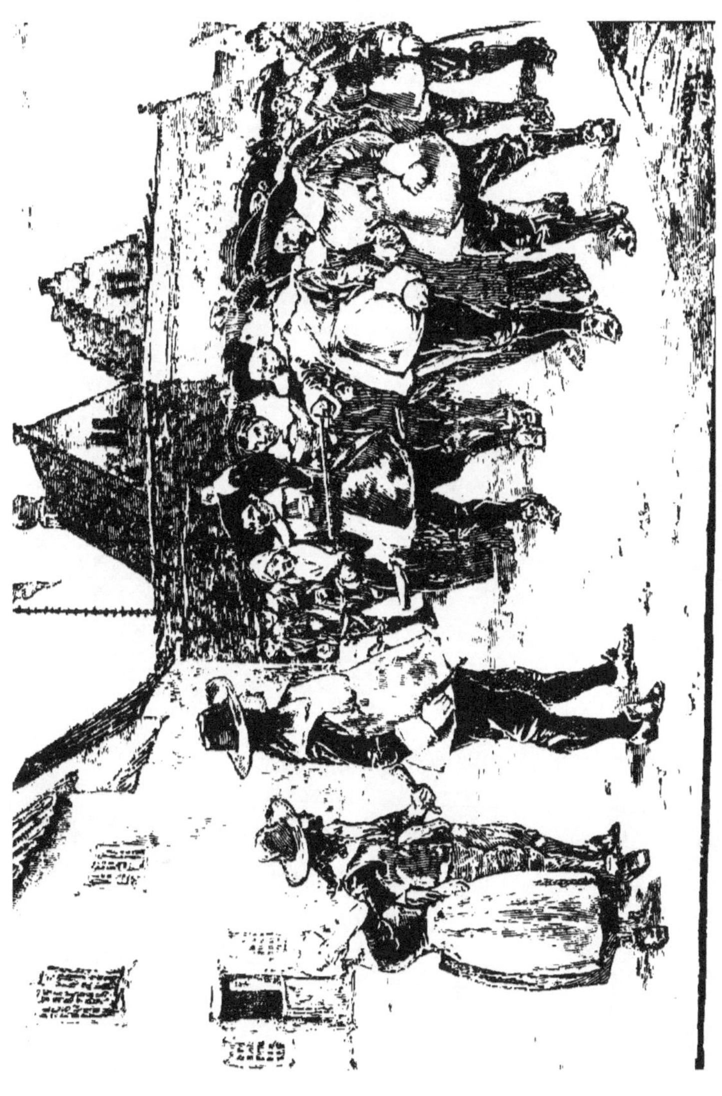

arrest and apprehension of the chief conspirators —
Colonel Bayard, the Heer Van Cortlandt, the Heer
Brockholdst, the Heer Pieter Jobse Marius, the
Worshipful Master Nicolls and the Worshipful
Master Reed. "Because that they had," so the
old warrant runs, "committed high misdemeanors
against His Majesty's authority in this province,
these are in His Majesty's King William's name
to will and require you to apprehend ye bodies of
ye said conspirators, wherever or in what place
soever they may be," etc., etc.

The Heer Van Cortlandt and most of those thus
apprehended managed to escape; but Colonel Bayard and Master Nicolls were not so fortunate.
They were hunted down and thrown into prison,
where the redoubtable Colonel soon regretted his
hot and rebellious acts and humbly sued for pardon. But this the Heer Governor did not feel himself able to grant.

But while these and other perplexities were filling
the days and nights of the Governor with care and
anxiety — made none the less perplexing by the
gloom and vindictive counsels of his friend and

chief adviser, the Heer Jacob Milborne, the boys
who served His Excellency as secretaries, or *Ge-
heimschryvers*, accompt-keepers, and messengers,
found ample sport and excitement in their work.
Rumors of French wars, of Indian disturbances, or
of home plots; risings in the country towns near
the city, where the farmers hearing of Bayard's attack on the Heer Governor and fearing for his
safety, as the old record states:

Flockt into the City, armed, in great numbers and notwith-
standing the Endeavours of the Magistrates to appease them
took the Liberty as is too usuall with an Enraged Multitude
and perpetrated Revenge on those which were ye Occasion
of their danger.

Perry, the post-rider, too, suffered the just pen-
alty of his treachery, and chafed under a wise restraint in the city prison; or, as the Heer Governor quaintly expressed it, " because that I have
found that myne letters have been broke open and
abused, I intend that you must keep me here company for a while."   And so it came to pass that
one sharp January morning young Abram Gouverneur set out as special post-rider in Perry's place,

to convey certain letters addressed to the Secretary of the Massachusetts Colony across the country to where riders from New Haven should receive and forward them. Likewise he had orders from the Heer Governor "to inform all honest and well-intended persons verbally what is passed" in the city. And, best of all, for the temporary rest and better security of the fair Mistress Mary the young *Geheimschryver* was commissioned to escort the Governor's daughter to the house of the good Sieur Bonnefoy, one of the Huguenot friends of the Heer Leisler, in the refugee settlement of New Rochelle.

Highly pleased with his triple mission and his pleasant company Abram set out with Barry Van Schaick as extra escort, with charming Mistress Mary well and warmly wrapped for her long ride. All three were well and safely mounted. It was a delightful winter's morning, crisp and clear, with the frozen snow crunching noisily under the horses' hoofs. And it was a still more delightful gallop as they went dashing northward along the old post-road that kept to the eastern side of the island about the line of the Bowery and Third

Avenue of to-day. On they scurried past pleasant-looking farms, white in their winter wraps, along the shore of the now frozen Fresh Water, across wide commons where in the months of grass the town herdsman, Gabriel Crapsey, armed with horn and staff, watched the city's cows, now climbing rocky and wind-swept hillsides and now through great stretches of dense woodland, where oak and chestnut and tamarack glistened in the sunlight with their overcoats of snow, then again through flat and well-kept farmlands, along the base of the *Slang Berg*, or Snake Hill (now Mount Morris), until at last they drew rein in front of the tavern of Johannes Verveelen, the ferryman, at the Wading or Wedding Place in the village of Nievw Haarlem and bade vrouw Verveelen set them across the river to the opposite, or Fordham shore.

Now she was a secret adherent of the Heer Van Cortlandt and the enemies of the Heer Governor. So rare a prize as the Heer Governor's daughter and the Heer Governor's Secretary did not fall into her hands every day, and she determined to make the most of her opportunity, and yet she must act cautiously. For she must not lose her place at the Ferry where she could work secretly and effectively against the Heer Governor, and she must not arouse the suspicions of her goodman the Heer Verveelen, who, though nearly eighty now, was still strong and hearty and the firm friend and supporter of the Heer Leisler.

"Nay, my fair mistress, and nay, my good secretary," she said with an excess of welcome, "such rare chance doth not come to us poor folk at the Wedding Place every day. 'Tis ebb tide now and the ice runs fast, but 'twill turn in a short half-hour and the flood will serve you best. So rest ye all awhile and taste my *beuelehn*,* and waffles and rullities, which I'll warrant me are nigh as good as goode vrouw Leisler's are. Come, 'twill be but a short half-hour and then the ice will serve you best for the ferrying."

Abram was for going straight on, but *beuelehn* and *rullities* were as a mighty magnet to the ever-hungry Barry and nice hot waffles and honey certainly had a strong attraction for Mistress Mary

* Fried hasty pudding with browned pork.

and the ice was running fast and the room did look
so cosey and inviting — and so Abram said "yes"
but added "a scant half-hour, mind you, goode
vrouw, for time, you know, is too precious to waste
at the flesh pots."

"Nay, good *Heer Gcheimschryver*," said the wily
goode vrouw, and Abram admitted to himself that
the title did sound grandly as she rolled it out;
"none know that more than I. See, you are
served," and as she spoke she piled their dishes
high, picking out the choicest dainties for hungry
Mistress Mary, even in the excess of her hospital-
ity going to the unaccustomed request that her
guest should " schmer botter oop de kook " (spread
butter on the cake). Then as the meal merrily
progressed, with laugh and joke between the three
young people, the goode vrouw slipped out, pleading household duties and an anxiety as to the tide,
and left her visitors to their meal in peace. The
half-hour was scarcely up when she once more appeared.

"The tide is on the turn," said she, "so now we
may set you safe across."

They led the horses on the lumbering flat-boat that lay at the ferry stairs.

"Where is the Heer Verveelen?" asked Abram, as he noted the absence of the old ferryman.

"He was fain to go to Van Keulen's Hook to view the stone bridge," replied the goode vrouw, as she pushed the boat into the current, "but Jan the soldier is as fair a ferryman as my own good man."

The ice cakes parted right and left as the clumsy boat drifted through them propelled by the pole of Jan, the soldier. But Abram's eye was watchful.

"Jan," he said suddenly, "'tis more a flood than I did think. Is not it bearing the boat somewhat out of course?"

Jan, the soldier, plied his pole and answered not a word. Abram repeated his question.

"Who is ferryman, master, you or I?" demanded Jan, the soldier, gruffly. "If that you think you can set us across more properly take the pole or else hold your peace, or I will not put you across."

"You will not!" exclaimed Barry hotly. "'Tis not what you will, but what we will, Master Jan."

"Is it not as I will ?   Aye, but it is," replied Jan, the soldier. "See now, pay me the ferry-rates or I go no further."

"Why, how now, Jan," said Abram. "Know you not we are on the Heer Governor's service, under special warrant and as such are exempt from ferry-rates. Push on now, on the Heer Governor's service."

"I know no Heer Governor," stoutly protested Jan, the soldier. "Old Heer Dog-Driver at the fort is no Governor for me. Pay me my rates or I will set you back."

The poles were out of water now and the ferry-boat borne by the strong current was drifting far from its course. Abram looked at Mary in some anxiety, but he was a lad of principle and felt that it would be wrong to give in.

"Do as I bid you, Jan," he demanded sternly, "and we will fix the rates hereafter. But on the Governor's service I may not pay you now."

"May not," growled Jan, the soldier, as with a mighty push he sent the boat hard against the Westchester shore, "then there be those who shall take full accompt from you." And as the ferry-boat grounded with a most demoralizing bump, Abram, glancing uneasily ashore, saw a group of men hurrying out from a clump of pines straight towards the stranded ferry-boat, and in their midst a mounted figure he knew only too well.

And then he knew his danger, and understood that he and his precious charge were foully and purposely betrayed into the hands of the enemy — the Heer Van Cortlandt and his men. What should he do?

CHAPTER XVII.

ABRAM acted quickly. There was need for rapidity both in thought and action.

"'Tis the king's business," he shouted at the approaching group. "Delay us not on your allegiance!"

But quick as was Abram in words Barry was even before him in deeds. With not an instant's delay he lowered his hard young head and, dashing at the unsuspecting and traitorous Jan, butted that much surprised ferryman so forcibly in the stomach as to double him completely up with the sudden shock and tumble him off the great flat-boat among the floating ice cakes of the fast-flowing Harlem. At the same time he wrenched the boat-pole from Jan's unsteady grasp and thrusting the extra pole into Abram's hand he cried excitedly, "Push off now, Abram; push off; push for dear life!"

Fear is a mighty impulse. Their young arms were filled with the strength of two young giants as they drove the poles into the ground; the flat-boat swung, with a surge, far into the stream and the travellers were out of harm's reach.

Jan the soldier picked himself up spluttering salt water and bad language with every breath, while the harsh voice of the baffled Heer Van Cortlandt called angrily from the shore: "Come back, come back, you young rapscallions, or it shall be the worse for you!"

Barry doffed his cap gracefully and bowed low to the Worshipful Ex-Mayor with a great show of politeness. Then he flung Scripture at him. "The king's business requireth haste," he shouted, as out into mid-stream he and Abram poled the clumsy ferry-boat.

They were safe in mid-stream, but in what a fix! The tide runs swiftly enough at the mouth of the Harlem river as any boy knows who has pulled a boat between the piers of the railroad bridge, or

tried to steady a crabbing float under the old
Third Avenue foot-bridge.   And to manage a lumbering flat-boat on which were three restive horses
and an equally excitable young girl in the midst
of a mass of floating ice was no easy matter, as
Abram and Barry soon discovered   Mary's fair
cheeks were flushed and her eyes were full of
action and eagerness.   For though anxious enough
as to the result, she was too brave a girl, too much
accustomed to danger and too deeply interested
in this latest adventure to have time for any such
unmaidenly quality as cowardice.   For girls are
not cowards, boys, though you may think it the
proper thing to say so.   In the supreme moment
of danger, history again and again has shown that
girls and women have faced without flinching what
boys and men have weakened and surrendered
under.   True bravery knows no sex.   And so,
when Barry — the reaction of their escape over —
looked at Abram inquiringly and Abram answered
with a dubious shake of the head, Mary spoke up
boldly.

"O boys," she cried earnestly, "'tis not for us

to give up now. We have — what is it the Heer Milborne doth say? — ah — we have them even as Samson had the Philistines; and we would fain smite them hip and thigh — by running away from them altogether," and Mistress Mary laughed merrily, even in the face of their great danger, at so pat an application of Scripture. " Push boldly over to the Harlem shore. Then may we land and, first heading townward to mislead them, turn then and gallop straight across the King's Bridge — the way we took, you mind it, Ab'm, last summer when we went to the Sieur Bonnefoy's, by that cross-road you both wot of."

"What, under Aspetong?" cried Barry altogether overpowered by Mary's suggestions.

" Sure; Aspetong!" echoed Abram. " Why did I not think of that? *Belle* Marie, you are fit to general the King's Majesty's own army. What a head you have, good faith!"

"And good faith, too," laughed Mary mockingly, " I need to have one when you two Worshipful Jonkheers have so lost yours. There, now have we struck, and see, they are watching us yet."

For while talking the boys had been poling as hard as they could and now the flat-boat had grounded on the low lands that lie along the south shore of the Harlem where the long line of boat-club houses now stand.

They led the horses off the boat and, quickly mounting, picked their way over the crusted snow, which, however, very often "slumped" badly under the horses' hoofs. The enemy, seeing them headed for Harlem village, hurried towards the ferry-landing to get across and intercept them, but the three fugitives, as soon as they were able to get on the townward side of a little rise of land and out of sight of their pursuers, turned their horses' heads and, floundering over the hard snow until they struck the central post-road, crossed the King's Bridge and were soon galloping, according to Mary's advice, along a fair road that would in time bring them under Aspetong.

Under Aspetong meant for them safety and help. For, under Aspetong, the high round hill that now overlooks the county town of Bedford and the lower sweeps of the beautiful valley of the Croton, were the winter wigwams and castle of the good Sakemacker Katonah, the father of Papaig and the friend of the Heer Leisler.

Katonah was a shrewd old savage. Not the highly poetical and altogether impossible red man of Cooper's stirring novels, nor the besotted, defrauded and dirty Western "red-skin" of to-day. Tall, brawny and well-made, with a countenance beaming at once with dignity and bear's grease, he was a powerful Sakemacker or sachem, and, as has been said, a shrewd old savage — shrewd enough to dispose of certain portions of his hunting grounds to the land-greedy Swannekens; shrewd enough to accumulate by this a goodly store of duffel-cloth, rum and Stroudwater blankets; and — while not forgetting that dreadful day many moons back when the false Swannekens under this very height of Aspetong* had fallen upon the castle and wigwams of his people and left one hundred and eighty Indians dead upon the blood-stained snow — shrewd enough to see that his long-held plans for vengeance lay not

* In February, 1644.

in useless warfare, but in stirring strife among the Swannekens themselves. And so he sided with the new Corlear,* the Heer Leisler, as against the old ones — the aristocrats, the sons of his fathers' murderers whom he hated heartily. And the old Sakemacker too was strong and shrewd enough to so become a part of history as to have his name live after him; † and to-day it marks one of the prettiest Westchester suburbs of New York on the line of the Harlem Railroad.

So he bustled out, dignified and stately with it all however, to meet and greet the young folks who came riding slowly towards the Indian village. "*Itah; itah!*" ‡ he said in welcome; and greeted by all the dogs and babies of the tribe in full and

---

*Corlear was the Indian title of the old Dutch governors, taken from Arendt Van Corlear, an early friend of the Indians.

† Here is the sign manual of the old-time and historic Indian sagamore taken from one of the old land records:

‡ "*Itah*"—good be to you—an Indian greeting.

AT THE WINTER WIGWAM OF KATONAH.

most unmusical chorus, and under escort of their friend, young Papaig, the travellers dismounted from their horses and entered the old Sakemacker's castle.

"My little brother shall go to the Corlear's friends at Shippa,"* he said, when Abram had related their story of adventure, "and no Swanneken from Schorakapak † to Shippa shall harm the *nitaps* ‡ of Katonah who have come to him under Aspetong for guiding and safety. Let the good Corlear's little daughter rest herself among the squaws of Katonah, and eat in peace of the *yolkeg* and *suckatash*.§ For she shall sleep in Mockea's own lodge and in the morning will Papaig and our braves see her safe to Shippa."

But when the young people had feasted well on the primitive Indian dishes, declining however the special tidbit of roast puppy as hardly to their taste, and when Mary carefully wrapped from the

---

* The old Indian name of New Rochelle.

† Indian name for "Spuyten Duyvel."

‡ Friend.

§ *Yolkeg* was a mush made of pounded parched corn, mixed with the juice of wild apples, and *suckatash* was made from corn and beans boiled together.

cold was sleeping snugly in old Mockea's lodge, Katonah said to Abram — for Barry, restless as ever, had gone with Papaig to indulge in the sport of *wigwass*,* by torchlight, through the ice :

"My little brother, here is grievous news to bear to my brother, the Corlear, at Manhatta. My runners have brought me this from Couxsachraga,"† and he drew from beneath his blanket a birch-bark scroll traced with rude signs and figures. Abram, though not skilled in Indian picture-reading, was deeply enough versed in woodland ways to know that the bark scroll indicated trouble in the Mohawk country. That wonderful-looking chapeau meant His Excellency, Count Frontenac the French Governor of Canada ; those rude guns were French soldiers, and the mass of tomahawks and scalps indicated an Indian foray on the border. But even while Abram bent over the scroll and the dignified old sagamore sought to explain its word of warning, a slight noise was heard without, the dogs barked loudly, the deer-

* "Bobbing eels" — almost any boy knows what that is.
† The New York wilderness around Fort Orange or Albany, now modernized into the Hudson River town of Coxsackie.

skin curtain of the lodge was thrust aside and a lithe Indian figure, naked save for the brief breech clout and short shoulder mantle of deerskin, entered with a swift and grave salute. The *Itah!* of welcome passed between the two savages and then Abram knew him as Mashato, Katonah's swiftest Indian runner, of whose marvellous trips and powers of endurance Papaig had told him.

"Mashato may speak the tidings. My little brother is the *nitap* of the Corlear at Manhatta," said Katonah as the runner looked warningly towards the white boy.

Mashato the runner gave his message: "Hear, O Katonah, our brothers of the wolf, beyond Couxsachraga send you swift and secret message. The French Corlear with the braves of the heron and the bear are on the war path. They have crossed the snows from beyond the great lake and taken heavy store of scalps with fire and ravage at Skaghneghtady."

"Skaghneghtady!" Abram caught at the word, through all Mashato's guttural speech. It was the Indian name for Schenectady, the little Dutch border village on the pine plains of the patroon's country, scarce twenty miles west of Albany. His heart almost stopped its beating. The Heer Governor, he knew, was even now seeking to extend his authority over the little palisadoed village and give it protection.

"Shinnectady!"—that was the old-time Dutch pronunciation of the word—"no, not Shinnectady!" he cried, hoping he might not have heard aright.

Mashato looked at him with unmoved face. "My little brother eateth Mashato's words," he said. "Mashato hath spoken true. The braves of the heron and the bear have taken every scalp in Skaghneghtady save some twoscore Swannekens who fled before the hatchet. Aramapow, the Onondaga runner, gave me the word direct."

"Katonah," exclaimed Abram energetically, "not a moment must be lost. This news must to the Heer Governor straight. I must ride back to the town this night. Will you, for the Corlear's sake, take brave care of his daughter, the Lady Marie, and see her safe to the Sieur Bonnefoy's at

Shippa after sun-up? Barry," he cried, as that young fisherman with a great string of slippery, squirming eels entered the lodge, "I must ride, as for life or death, to the Heer Leisler to-night. Shinnectady is laid waste and all our people are scalped. The French Indians are on the war-path and Fort Orange may go next and mayhap our own towns. Do you see to *belle* Marie. Katonah will give you safe escort and " —

"Nay, nay, A'bm," broke in the impetuous Barry, with the love of hazard and adventure ever strong in his stout young heart, " rather let me ride with the news to the town and do you look after the Lady Mary. She would like it better, I know, and I am the swiftest rider. You can give me the lines to the Heer Governor. You have your ink-horn and, see, here is a fair piece of white birch. Let me go. I know every morgen of land between here and the Copake and can make it by morning with my eyes shut. 'Twere better thus; it were indeed."

Barry's advice seemed wise, all things considered, and Abram, hastily explaining the situation to Barry and noting the same for the Heer Leisler as well as he was able on his birch-bark scroll, despatched Barry on the fleetest of the three horses to bear to the Heer Governor and the council the direful news that the Northern border was in danger, that the French Indians were on the war path and that Schenectady was in ruins — the story of that sad and bloody day that for full two hundred years has thrown a special interest around the name and history of the now prosperous city on the beautiful Mohawk.

CHAPTER XVIII.

SO Barry rode to town. Out into the wintry gloom and blackness he rode, where the scarcely broken pathway stretched through the crisp and starless night away towards the sleeping city full thirty miles to the south. The snow flew sharply from his horse's hoofs as he galloped on bearing his message of danger. With one hand on his ready pistol and one on his bridle rein, with eyes strained hard to pierce the gloom, and ears alert to catch the manifold noises of the night, right on he rode. Over wide wastes of ghostly, wind-swept commons, and up steep rises of hill; through long stretches of forest, dense and dark, where the wind moaning through the swaying tree-tops seemed voices of warning or of threatening, and the long *hoo-hoo* of the owl, answered to the quavering yelp of the gray wolf and the even more fearful screech of the "painter" or wild cat, still on and on he rode — fearing none of these so much as man's interference or an enemy's delay, on and on along all the fair river-land now thronged with the populous towns of Southern Westchester, on and on, along the ice-bound Bronx and across the King's Bridge, and over the Harlem Flats, until at last with horse nigh-spent, spite of all his cheering words and encouraging caresses, he drew rein and stopped his horse, all panting and reeking, before the dark "stoope" of the Halfway house, near where is now the corner of 109th street and Eighth Avenue.

"Yoho! so, yoho Corneel! Cornelis Jansen. Yo, hillo there! Help in the name of the King! Wake up; wake up! Fresh horse here for the Heer Governor's business! Soho; hillo! wake up, I say!"

Sleepy Cornelis Jansen, the thrifty innkeeper, thinking the Indians must sure be at his doors or, worse yet, that King James and the French mun-seers were sweeping up from town, tumbled from his bed and popped his nightcapped head warily through the open window.

"*Ach* — yah — hillo" — not yet really awake —

"SO BARRY RODE TO TOWN."

"who rouseth honest folk in such — so; 'tis but a jonkheer.   Pouf, so; what fool's trick is this?"

"Nay, no trick, Cornelis; 'tis I, Barry Van Schaick, riding on matters of life or death to the

Heer Governor. My horse is spent and I must have another, for I must be in the Strand by dawn. The French king's Indians are up and massacring, and I must bear the tidings straight to town."

"Massacring!" yelled Cornelis, now fully roused, popping his white head into the room again. "Massacring!" Barry heard the shrill shriek of the goode vrouw Jansen echo, and soon two pair of sturdy Dutch feet came clattering down the heavy stairs and straight to the tavern door. In an instant he was forced within and beseeched for his story. But he had told it all. "So run the tidings," he said when he had given them his details, " and now on your allegiance I charge you see me freshly horsed and let me be off anon."

And now he is in saddle again and flying towards the town on Cornelis Jansen's swiftest horse. Down the *Konaande Kough* or King's Highway, over the old post-path later known as the Bloomingdale Road, over hill and through woodland where now stretch the beautiful meadows of the great Central Park, across snow-covered dale and broad common the young messenger rides fast. The sleepy warders at the Land Gate have scarce time to unbar the rickety postern at the call of "In the King's name!" and to rub their eyes in bewilderment, when through the open gate and straight down the Broad Way, flashes a vision of a stout boy on a galloping gray. There is a shout of "To the Heer Governor. On the king's business!" and horse and boy are gone. And so the night-ride ends and in the gray of the winter's morning Barry Van Schaik draws rein before the well-known door on the Strand, and the Heer Governor knows that Schenectady has been sacked and that all the northern border, which he trusted to hold for the king, is in danger.

Jacob Leisler was a man of prompt and energetic action. Only thus had he been able to instil his sturdy ideas of liberty and the rights of the citizen into the slow-going burghers of Manhattan, and only thus, now, could he hope to thwart the designs of the French enemies of the province and the plottings of traitors within his own borders. For months past the little town of Albany, the main defence and reliance of the northern frontier, had denied his right to rule as governor, had openly opposed his commands and defied his messengers. The little fur-trading station felt its own importance as an outlying station of the King's provinces and asserted its independence alike of patroon and governor, and the Heer Leisler had been greatly perplexed how to act in regard to the obstinate little town. But there must be no hesitation now. The safety of the entire province and the authority of His Majesty the King were of more importance than the petty feuds as to who was chief ruler. Barry's plucky night-ride had shown him to be a quick and reliable messenger and he was despatched post-haste to Captain Milborne at Fort Orange, bidding him enter the town and prepare for its proper defence. But ere he could reach the gates the Albany burghers in the terror of the Schenectady massacre had seen where their true safety lay and had received the Heer Governor's representatives in the town and acknowledged his authority. Jacob, Jr., now a wise young lieutenant was hurried off to Governor Treat, of the Connecticut colony, with information of the disaster and an appeal for help against the common foe, and young Abram Gouverneur was taken into the Heer Governor's Council for the necessary assistance as secretary.

The debate in council, which met that day at the Heer Alderman Walter's house on the Hoogh Straat,* was short and sharp as to what should be done. Instant relief must be despatched to the border — that was certain. Already the Heer Governor's fierce and unscrupulous enemies were seeking to fix the responsibility of the Schenectady massacre upon him, and no one knew what baser methods they might use to poison the people against him.   Further than this, so said good Heer Mayor Delanoy, "'twere wiser, Heer Governor, not to proceed. We have our own town's safety at stake. We must defend it from the Papists and the French munseers from over sea; and who will not look to provide for his own and specially for those of his own house, so sayeth Holy Writ, hath denied the faith and is worse than an infidel."

But Jacob Leisler was above selfish measures.

* High street, now Stone street near Hanover Square.

"You do rightly quote the Holy Writ, Heer Mayor," he said, "but, so please you, I doubt lest you give it not a broad enough expounding. For see you not that they of Albany and the north are surely of our own house and need our strongest arm. Trust me, the Count Frontenac seeketh to wrest these northern provinces from the King's Majesty for the glory of the French King, his master. This matter of Shinnectady is but his first blow. Who then shall save this our home land for our Gracious Sovereign? We must, Heer Mayor! We must and will! And how better than by marching straightway into Canada and striking the enemy on his own ground?"

Invade Canada! It almost took the breath away from those slow debating burghers. The plan was altogether too gigantic for them to contemplate. The members of the Council started in surprise and looked at the Heer Governor, fearful that the troubles on the border and in the town had turned his brain. But there he sat cool and calm.

"We must march into the French king's country or our own will be his spoil," he repeated.

"But, Heer Governor," said the Heer Mayor Delanoy when he had recovered his breath, "how may this rash thought be compassed? Surely our little province may never look to cope with the men of war of King Louis and the Count Frontenac."

"Mighty hosts have even been overcome by little ones," said the Heer Governor; and then growing still more thoughtful he added, "if now but the Connecticut colony would but join our enterprise we might make a fairer show of force."

There was a brief silence. Then Abram Gouverneur, the young secretary who was quietly noting the actions of the council, said: "Pardon, Heer Governor, but why might not all the colonies of the king join you in this matter? 'Tis for the common defence."

The Heer Governor struck the table a mighty blow with his clenched fist. "The Jonkheer is right," he exclaimed joyfully. "Let all the colonies join for the common safety and then who shall hope to withstand us! Friends, 'tis wisely spoken. Let us to the work at once."

And so it came to pass that, after one hundred

and sixty men had been sent for the immediate succor of Albany and the frontier, letters were sent to the governors of all the northern provinces, proposing a union of council for the general good. The proposition met with favor, and on the first day of May, 1690, the first Continental Congress ever convened in America assembled in the city of New York in the council chamber of the old Stadt Huys in Coenties Slip. The rough stones of that quaint old building, long ago demolished, are now a part of the foundations of many an old warehouse of lower New York ; but, even as they have been built into the business structures of the now mighty city, so the principles of helpfulness and comradeship put into practical effect by that first Continental Congress — of which history says but little and your school-books nothing whatever — helped to the development of those principles which made this great union of free States possible. And thus, even before the patriots of the Fourth of July and the Revolution, a still earlier patriot — Jacob Leisler, the first " people's governor " in these colonies — laid the corner-stone of the American Union and paved the way for the Declaration and the Revolution.

Five colonies were directly represented in this Congress — New York, Massachusetts, Connecticut, Plymouth and Maryland.   Rhode Island promised aid, New Jersey favored the enterprise, Virginia said but little and Pennsylvania, " land of the Quakers," declared it as " ag't their prin'cls " to fight; therefore when " ye ffrench come they are intended to send some of their wisest people to tell them that rather would they give up their land and goods than to fight "— so runs the old record.   The invasion of Canada was decided upon and eight hundred and fifty-five men were at once promised as the first grand army of the United Colonies!

But Mary, thinking little of all these important matters — after a speedy return from the Sieur Bonnefoy's at New Rochelle— spent the long summer in quiet, helpful ways at home.   And, while Barry was spurring in one direction and Jacob, Jr., in another; while Abram was deep in matters of council and congress, and the Heer Milborne was in-

sisting that he, and not Winthrop of Massachusetts, should be generalissimo of the colonial forces
in the North; while the Count Frontenac, the Canadian Governor, and his savage Indian allies
were watching every movement of the hated English, and the colonists, divided among themselves,
were full of quarrels and jealousies which made
the Heer Governor sick at heart and almost hope-
less as to the success of his great plan; while the
people were grumbling at the fear of a war tax,
and the Heer Governor's three privateers were
scouring the New England waters on the watch
for French ships; while the beautiful Northern
summer filled the land with greenness and glory
from the Thousand Islands of the broad St. Lawrence to the little rondel or half-moon forts that
looked seaward to Staten Island and the Bay, fair
Mistress Mary went her homely ways and did her
simple duties, full of anxiety and yet of hope for
her father's success, but saying little, as was the
custom with young folks in those strict old days.

Thus matters stood when at the close of one
glorious September day the goode vrouw Leisler,

placing a hand on Mary's golden head said quietly :
" My daughter, are you not ever ready to obey your
father's commands when they are for your welfare
and the public good ? "

Mary looked into her mother's serious face, surprised and startled at so curious and unexpected a
question, and asked, " Have I ever failed you, or
my father ? "

" Never, my Mary," Mother Leisler replied.
" And now indeed cometh a test of all your obedience — though, sooth to say, such a matter should
smack less of obedience than of joyousness.   What
think you of the Heer Milborne, child ? "

" What think I of the Heer Milborne, mother ? "
said Mary, repeating her mother's query with still
more of surprise and curiosity on her face.   " Why
do you ask ?   Why — good faith, mother, I — I
never think of him ! "

" Then settle your thoughts more worthily upon
him and his favors, my daughter," said her mother
soberly ; " for it is your father's will and my desire
that you do wed with the Heer Milborne ere yet
the spring returns."

CHAPTER XIX.

KING STORK.

MARRY the Heer Milborne! Mary's fair cheek flamed hotly at the thought and something of her father's spirit flashed in her blue eyes and then as quickly died away in a look of piteous protest.

"O mother!" was all she said.

The goode vrouw Leisler stood silent, watching and waiting. Then Mary's speech came back and she exclaimed, "Marry the Heer Milborne! I? Why, mother, I am far too young a maid even to think of wedding yet."

"*Ach!* hear the child," said Mother Leisler with a look of forced good humor on her anxious face. "That is but folly, girl. Why, I was less your age, scarce fourteen, good faith, when I married the worshipful Heer Pieter Vanderveer, my first good-

man, in the old Loockermans house you know so well
by the fort.   And I could point you out goode vrouws
in plenty in this little town who were wives — aye,
and widows — before your age, daughter."

"But the Heer Milborne!" exclaimed Mary,
routed on her first argument, "why, mother, I do
not even like the man. Nay, more, I do much dislike him."

"A mere matter of fancy, child," her mother
said. "Loving comes in time, trust me for that.
Few of our marriages are aught but grounded on
need ; love scarce entereth in ; and who should be
the wiser judge of what is best for you — your
father and mother or your own silly self who knoweth not your own mind ? It must be as we say, child,
not as you wish."

And true enough this was the stern and harsh
doctrine of those hard old days when the father's
will was law and the tendernesses of home were
neither many nor strong.   Thank heaven, for these
later and better days of ours when the home has
more of love even if it has also more of indulgence,
and when parents and children are comrades and

lovers rather than autocrats and serfs. And yet the Leisler home was as happily constituted a one as any in the old Dutch days, and Mary loved her stern father as did he her — so strongly in fact that he, who dared face the hottest foe, dared not face the protest of his own daughter.

Rebellion is the last resort against tyranny. The Leisler blood was up, and even in Mary's quiet young life when the will grew strong it could stand firm against all odds.

"Nay, mother," she said, setting her teeth firmly together and speaking with slow determination, "nay, mother, I will *not* marry the Heer Milborne; I say I will not!"

The goode vrouw Leisler turned upon her daughter, but not with the look of stern severity that might have been expected to follow such an outburst of rebellion. She placed her hand tenderly on the girl's fair head and spoke quietly:

"Mary, child, you love your father, do you not? Nay, answer me not" — as Mary strove to speak — "wait, rather, till I have ceased. You love your father and have ever been the first to echo his strong words as to what each man and woman, ay, and the tiniest child may do for the sake of country and the King's High Majesty. You have wished that you were a lad that you might do something or give, mayhap, your life to help the cause of the people. Here is your chance, my daughter. *Give yourself!* Your father, sore perplexed by the trials and tribulations of the time, hath entrusted to the Heer Milborne certain grave and secret matters which none but he should know. And the Heer Milborne now maketh your hand the hostage for your father's faith. He hath it in his power, should he so decide, to aid or to ruin, not alone your father, but the cause of the people which your father holdeth dearer than his own life even. 'Tis a solemn compact, child, between them both ; and what are young maids' foolish hearts when matters of life or death impend ? Shame not your father's word nor mine, my daughter, by unseemly refusal, and, above all, shame not your own vows by now refusing to give yourself for your country's good when the demand for giving cometh to you as now."

It was a bitter dilemma and one that in these happier days could scarce come into the life and heart of a fair young maid of fifteen. But to Mary it had a deep and strong significance. She felt the force of her mother's words and the pressure of her father's needs. Strangely enough she did not think to question the harsh selfishness of the Heer Milborne's alternative.

"Mother, let me consider; let me be alone with myself," was all she said. And then slowly, with drooping head and downcast eyes, she sought her own little chamber that looked across the flowing river to the Breuckelen hills. She thought over the matter calmly and sorrowfully. She thought of the Heer Milborne; of her father and her mother, but oftenest of Abram. Poor Abram!

For these two young people — Abram and Mary —growing up together in a pleasant boy and girl comradeship now stood on the threshold of young manhood and womanhood with that comradeship blossoming into a still stronger and more enduring affection. Abram had ever been Mary's ready champion and protector; Mary had always proven

SHE THOUGHT OVER THE MATTER CALMLY AND SORROWFULLY.

herself Abram's loving helper and true and loyal friend. And what are these but qualities that ripen into stronger affections, the memories of which help to brighten life and fill it with tender recollections however its paths divide? We laugh over our boy and girl attachments and call them childish follies, but is it not wiser to cherish rather than to ridicule them? Life is too full of bitterness to forego one such touch of gracious and trusting loyalty — one such store of happy and helpful memories.

And so she thought oftenest of Abram — of Abram now far away chasing after French ships on one of the Heer Leisler's privateering brigantines — and she said, " Oh! if only he were here to give me advisement; what would he say? What indeed? Hath he not told me many a time and oft the stories which his uncle Heer Patem the captain did tell him of the brave Huguenots and how they dared everything for the religion? And of the great admiral and how he said to his sons : ' There is one thing more a man has to give — it is the last thing — it is his life?' And if a man, why not a maid?

What is my life to me more than was theirs to them? 'Tis my duty to make this sacrifice — even for Ab'm's sake."

And so it came to pass that, when this idea of sacrifice needed and duty to be done was firmly fixed in her loving young heart, she came down the broad stairway to the living room and, placing her hand in her mother's, said simply, " It shall be, mother, even as you wish."

And then the motherly heart of the goode vrouw Leisler — tender and motherly in spite of her strong views on the duty and obedience of children — overflowed completely, and she took Mary to her heart with tears and caresses.

And soon the news of Mary's consent spread abroad. It came to the Heer Leisler, perplexed and care-worn in his thronging worries of office and he only laid his broad hand on Mary's golden head and said, " My brave daughter!" It came to the Heer Milborne stern and contentious in Albany town where he was hurrying the colonial troops northward and striving with Winthrop and the New England leaders for the chief command, and he simply sent to Mary a brief and formal letter of approval and advice that sorely tried the young maid's temper. It came to Jacob, Jr., bustling in all his new authority of a lieutenant in the train-bands — in the camp at Wood Creek on the northern shores of Lake Champlain where the troops of the colonies, a prey to dissensions, lack of provisions and the small-pox, waited for the word of advance on Canada — and, brother-like, he only said briefly, "What! Mary marry old gruff-and-grum? Poor Mary!" It came to Barry, fleet messenger for the Heer Governor speeding eastward with appeals for instant help for the army in the North; and it so stirred that young courier that he waylaid Abram cruising, as representative of the Heer Governor with the New York privateers, to join Sir William Phipps and his fleet at Boston. And so at last it came to Abram. "Marry the Heer Milborne!" he said, while his face grew red and hot. "O Barry, 'tis sure not possible!" But when he knew that it was the truth, and when furthermore with his knowledge of Mary's sense of duty and honor and of how matters stood with her father, he could understand her reasons for such a decision, he only said, " Poor *belle* Marie ; 'tis a sorry sacrifice of a tender young life, and I who have ever talked boastfully to her of devotion to duty am shamed by her action.   But, oh ! it should not be."

At this Barry was greatly disgusted.   For that hot-headed young partisan had counted on Abram's sudden and indignant rebellion, and looked forward to a wonderfully great adventure — nothing less than a midnight abduction of Mistress Mary by himself and Abram, a retreat to Katonah's wigwams under Aspetong, a swift journey to the coast and escape in one of the brigantines to the eastern colonies where Abram and Mary might be safe from the Heer Governor's tyranny and the Heer Milborne's schemes.

Yes, the Heer Governor's tyranny.   It had come to that even with loyal Barry.   For day by day and month by month the people were growing more critical of the very man they had placed in power.   The secret work of the Heer Van Cortlandt and other bitter enemies of the Heer Leisler, though at first indignantly repelled by the popu-

lace, was gradually developing into open or danger·
ous opposition, and the plots against him that had
been planned beyond the gates were gradually
gaining foothold within the walls. And now came
the sorry ending of his cherished plan for the brilliant conquest of Canada by the united colonies —
a defeat and failure brought about by the miserable strife for leadership in the camp, the cowardly
weakening of his authority with the troops by his
bitter enemies, and the utter incompetence of the
men selected as officers in command. The troops
came home sick and dispirited, and Canada was
not won — it was not even invaded. Sir William
Phipps and his fleet returned from Quebec storm·
tossed and without spoil, and now the bills must
be paid. People do not grumble at having to pay
for success, but to pay for failure is a far different
matter. So when the Heer Governor had to tax
the New Yorkers to get the money to pay for their
failure they commenced to growl and grumble
angrily enough against the man who had sought to
act only for their good. A year before they had
called him the " savior of the province " and " the

people's friend," but now — while he was "Heer Governor" to his face — behind his back he was "Lieutenant Blockhead," "Deacon Jailer," "Governor Dog-driver," and such angry nicknames. Do any of my young readers remember old Æsop's fable of King Log and King Stork? Well, the brave Heer Leisler was now a regular King Stork to his former worshipers. Ah! boys and girls, if you read history carefully, you will learn that those who have striven hardest for their fellow men have been the most maligned; that nothing is so unpopular as failure; that nothing succeeds like success. And, to crown it all, there came a stormy winter's-day in the early year, January 29, 1691, when Barry who had been across to Staten Island to serve notices of forfeit against certain delinquent tax-payers, burst into the council-room in the Fort where Abram sat busily writing, and cried excitedly:

"News, news, Ab'm — and sorry news at that! Here be word that one of the king's ships hath just past the Hoofden and even now lies at anchor off the Nutten in which cometh a captain from the

King's Majesty who, folk say, will thrust the Heer Governor from his station and give the power again to the Papists and aristocrats."

And, scarce had he ceased speaking when the quick stroke of oars came from the water side and a boat's crew from the ship *Beaver* now riding at anchor off Nutten Island, came to the fort from the landing, demanding from the Heer Jacob Leisler — "self-styled Lieutenant-Governor and Commander-in-chief of His Majesty's Province of New York" — an instant and entire surrender "to Major Richard Ingolsby, of His Majesty's Regiment of Foot, of His Majesty's Fort in the name and for the behalf of our Sovereign Lord and Lady King William and Queen Mary, the peace of their crown and the dignity and safety of this their Province of New York!"

CHAPTER XX.

'TWIXT HAWK AND BUZZARD.

A FINE to-do, good faith!" cried Barry, hot-faced and indignant when he heard Major Richard Ingolby's surprising message. "What doth it all mean, Ab'm?"

For Barry had been absent so much of late on special business for the Heer Governor that these new complications were a mystery to him, and he had only the unfounded gossip of the town to lead him — where gossip generally leads — into still deeper perplexity. And so while the messengers were conducted to the presence of the Heer Leisler, Abram briefly explained the case to Barry. He told him how the news had come from England of the triumph of the Heer Governor's enemies in the King's court, through false tales and representations, and how the king had appointed the Heer Colonel Henry Sloughter as Governor of His Majesty's Province of New York and admiral of all the seas adjoining, and how even now the new Governor was on the way with ships and soldiers to take full posession.

"And is then our own Governor to be set aside?" queried Barry indignantly.

"So it seemeth," Abram replied, "for the word of the people goeth but for little when the grandees desire it otherwise. But, truth to tell, the Heer Leisler is ready to bow to the decree of the King's Majesty and give up the ruling of the Province to this new Governor whom the king doth send, knowing that his own power cometh rather from the people than from the King's Grace and that it was to span the time between the flight of old King James and his Governor, Nicholson, and the Governor of the new King's Majesty, the Prince of Orange. But, because he holdeth the governorship till such time, he may not lightly give it up to any one who may demand it without showing the king's order so to do, the which this Heer Major Ingolsby not having, he may not properly expect nor demand the surrender of the king's fort."

The unsupported and headstrong demand of Majoy Ingolsby, as Abram intimated, had only led to more puzzling complications. Scarce had his ship, the *Beaver* (which had reached New York in safety, while the other vessels of the fleet conveying Colonel Sloughter and his troops had been driven by stress of weather to the Bermudas), dropped anchor below Nutten — now Governor's — Island, than the chief enemies of the Heer Leisler hurried on board and placing their false version of the troubles in the Province before Major Ingolsby had speedily won to their side this high-tempered and quarrelsome English officer who could not acknowledge any good in aught that the people might do. Hence his insolent message to the Heer Leisler — a message altogether unwarranted inasmuch as he had neither the right nor the power to make it, having no authority from the King nor from Governor Sloughter so to do. And even as Abram concluded his explanations to Barry this was still further proven, as in the open doorway of the council chamber the two messengers of the

English Major appeared followed courteously by the Heer Leisler who said :

" And so, gentlemen, although I would willingly resign and transfer the possession of His Majesty's fort to the Heer Ingolsby were it proper for me so to do, I must, in the absence of any papers showing his right to make the demand, flatly decline. Bear my respects to his honor, the Heer Major, and say that all good offices and accommodations for the King's troops in this his loyal town of New York shall be cheerfully granted; but for the transfer of this fort and the munitions of the King's Majesty in this Province I must await the arrival and the authority of the Heer Colonel Sloughter."

It was a wise and logical decision, but it had a sorry result. Major Ingolsby, angered and wrathful at being thus braved by a mere civilian, grew all the more obstinate and determined, and the enemies of the Heer Leisler became more furious in their charges and more bitter in their advice. On the other hand the people of the town, divided in opinion and knowing that a new Governor had been appointed in the Heer Leisler's place, sought to

avoid trouble and complications by the most cowardly of all methods, a surrender of principles, a
spiritless giving up of all that they had gained, and
basely counselled their duly appointed Governor
to give over his authority to an unauthorized power
rather than to create any trouble or annoyance.
There are just such people, boys and girls, in all
critical times, safe-side men who will submit to any
thing rather than have their own affairs disturbed.

And so, 'twixt hawk and buzzard, as the old
hunters call such a position, the Heer Leisler stood
firm and unmoved, conscious that he was right and
determined to be true to the trust the people had
given him and loyal to his superior, the King.

And in the midst of it all, one dull February day
a quiet wedding — a sombre wedding — took place
in the ugly house on the Strand — a wedding at
which many of the family friends and most of the
customary merry-making of the old Knickerbocker
weddings were absent, and blue-eyed Mary Leisler,
whom all the town had loved, became the vrouw
Mary Milborne, while all the town wondered how
such a thing could be and even added that to their

growing dislike of their once popular Governor. And Abram, poor Abram, who, brave young fellow though he was, had thus far said not a word, because he felt that he knew the reason for Mary's sacrifice, broke down at the last, and begged that he might be sent far away on that dismal wedding-day. And the Heer Governor, as if he knew his thoughts, granted his wish. And so it came to pass that Abram spent Mary's wedding-day pacing the beach and the headlands at the Sandy Hook watching the sea for some sign of Governor Sloughter's long-expected ships.

But the Heer Governor Sloughter came not; the days hurried on, and the position of affairs in the fort and in the town were growing more and more critical. Major Ingolsby and his troops, entering the city, were quartered in the old Stadt Huys, at Coenties Slip, volunteers to help drive out the "rebels," as he termed the Heer Leisler's followers were called for, while the Heer Leisler, on the other hand, publicly protested against Major Ingolsby's acts and called on the neighboring militia to rally to his support. The soldiers on

both sides were boisterous and unruly, public senti-
ment ran high among the people and everything
was ripe for an outbreak. The Heer Leisler alone
preserved his calmness and determination, and
while protesting against the words and acts of his
opponents, counselled moderation, and begged that
they should all quietly await the coming of the new
governor, who should set matters right.

So in threats and protests, in demands and
counterdemands, in anxiety and expectation the
winter wore away. The king's troops, swelled by
accessions from the mass of the weak-kneed, the
discontented and the openly hostile ones in the
province, now mustered in large force, and held
available sections of the town, while the Heer Governor's opposing force of some three hundred men
of the train-bands were crowded in the fort, save
where a small portion of the burgher-guard held
the rude Block-house in the Smits Vly.

It was March 17th, 1691 ; one of those few days
full of glorious sunshine and the promise of the
spring, that occasionally come in that worst month
of the year and make the broad bay of New York

a dazzling picture of blue water and of bluer skies. On one of the bastions of the little fort stood our three friends, Abram, Jacob, Jr., and Barry, not studying the landscape beauties of this rare March morning but, all angry and anxious, looking out

THE OUTLOOK FROM THE FORT.

towards the town where across the head of the Broad Way and of the Winckel street rose the rough earthworks which Major Ingolsby's men had hastily thrown up and which commanded both the sally port and the fort walls.

"Plague take the pestilent fellows!" broke out Jacob, Jr., furious at the sight; "if but now my father would listen to my words we might soon scat-

ter yon insolents and see who is master in the **town.**
I am half-minded to do it myself."

The idea of a battle on one's own hook struck
Barry as peculiarly attractive. "Why not, Jacob?"
he cried excitedly. "There be an hundred and
more good fellows in the fort here will follow you.
We could easily scatter yon red-coats and hold
their dirt heaps for the Heer Governor's use,
and, good faith, why should we not *over-loopen* the
walls and get the best of them? We are held so by
the nose here that we may neither send out for
succor nor get in even **bread** to eat ere long. So
what should stay us from one bold stroke, say I?"

"Nothing indeed, save your own good sense and
the Heer Governor's word," replied Abram. "'Tis
life and dea h to his plans to make no move which
yon insolents there can twist to talk of treason
against the King's Majesty, and what else would
such a crazy dash as this your counsel be?"

"What indeed?" said a deep voice; and turning in some dismay the three young fellows saw
the Heer Leisler himself standing behind them.

"Good faith, young folk," he said, "were it not

for Ab'm's wiser speech, blood and treason would both run riot in this unhappy town. 'Tis hard enough to hold our train-band men in check. Let not my own kith and kin help on the bitter feud by bloody talk and threat."

And as Jacob, Jr., and Barry, a trifle shamefaced at this merited rebuke, walked quickly away the Heer Governor, laying a hand on Abram's arm said slowly but forcibly, "Ab'm lad, when that these troubles did first commence and you were but a lad I once did counsel caution and said to you, 'none knoweth how these troubles may end!' Alas, see how they bid fair to end"—and he pointed sorrowfully at Major Ingolsby's hostile earthworks. "For full six weeks now have the Heer Ingolsby and his traitorous abettors held us in siege and stress, the people are slowly falling away from their own brave stand, and I can only wait the arrival of the King's Governor and the orders of the King's Grace."

"Yet surely, Heer Governor," said Abram, some of Barry's and Jacob's desires still firing his heart, "surely you have with you enough of good men and true both within and without this fort to uphold your word and will. If that you would bid us to force this matter to the test I'll warrant me that yon insolent Englishman and his treacherous aids shall go flying out of their dirt-heaps and beyond the city gates."

The Heer Leisler shook his head. "'Tis not to be thought of, Ab'm," he replied. "Not to save my own life would I of my own act, end this affair in blood. I must bide my time till the Heer Colonel Sloughter doth appear, when I will gladly resign the power which the people have given me. Till then, come what may, I will hold firmly to my purpose and am not to be turned aside by yon blustering and traitor insolents. But, good faith, they try me to the top of my temper! Only last night did they dare to forbid my proclamation in the town by beat of drum, and to patrol their guard to the very gates of His Majesty's fort. But that 'tis my need to hold myself in check, I would take them roundly to task in more stern and harmful guise than in the solemn protest which I would have you write for me this day."

He waited a moment and looked across at the enemy's moving lines and great show of parade. Then he said, "'Twere wiser, since I am so fell a mark of enmity to my foes, that mine own household should be guarded from ill in time. Ab'm," and he faced his young companion suddenly, "do you, this very day, take Mary for better safety to our Huguenot friends at New Rochelle."

Abram looked at the Heer Governor in sheer amazement. It was the first time Mary's name had been mentioned between them since her dreary wedding-day.

"What, Heer Governor," he cried with French impetuosity, "*I* take *belle* Ma — I mean rather the vrouw Milborne to New Rochelle? *I*, said you? Why should not the Heer Milborne himself take his — dame —" But the Heer Leisler placed his hand on Abram's arm, as if he read his thoughts. "Ab'm, my son," he said gently, "ask nought, but act. Have done with 'vrouws' and 'dames.' Think only of your playfellow of fairer days. Will you not shield and save my daughter — your sister?"

All the chivalric promptings of his French ancestry tingled in the lad's veins. "Heer Governor," he said earnestly, "I will die for you—for—Marie! Bid me go when and where you will and if I fail—well—here's my head. That shall be the forfeit of my failure!"

But ere he could leave the fort to do this singular bidding of his patron a stronger force interfered and Mary Milborne did not find the safety her father planned for her that fair March day, in the friendly custody of her Huguenot friends of New Rochelle. For that very afternoon, before Abram could steal out through the Water Gate to the Leisler *bouwerie* where horses for the journey awaited them, the sharp and sudden sound of musketry awoke the startled town. Across the open space that lay beyond the Winckel street came Barry Van Schaick running for dear life, a gun on the ramparts of the little fort boomed out a reply, and the storm so long dreaded had burst at last. The battle of New York had begun.

CHAPTER XXI.

BARRY STIRS THINGS UP.

OF course Barry was at the bottom of it all.
It seemed consistent that a revolution begun
by a boy's heedlessness should be brought to a
head by a boy's recklessness.   For it so happened
that when the hot-blooded young fellows had turned
away from the Heer Leisler's reproof on the bastion
of the fort, Jacob, Jr., and Barry had parted company and the latter hearing from one of the town's-
people who had slipped past the English sentries
that a large amount of provisions for the garrison
were gathered on the Breuckelen beach awaiting the
darkness for shipment across the river, declared his
readiness, if but two other hardy spirits would join
him, to bring across a boatload in broad daylight
in face of the English guards.   For fresh provisions
had a marvellous attraction for Barry Van Schaick.

The hardy spirits were not lacking. Louwerens (Lawrence) Ackerman and big Dirck Ryckman, the miller's son, volunteered at once, and soon the three had sprung into an open boat and pulled across to the sandy beach below the Breuckelen heights.

There, sure enough, they found a goodly store of provender sent by the friendly farmers of Long Island for the Heer Governor Leisler's needs, and loading a choice supply in their boat they started for the fort again. But how often is the coming back far, far different from the going forward. Any one who to-day watches at the prow of a Brooklyn ferry boat, or from the centre of the big bridge, cannot fail to note the fearful rush of the flood tide in the East river from the Atlantic docks, to Kip's Bay, and will know that a loaded row boat fares but hardly in trying to lay a straight course across the river from the Fulton Ferry to Coenties Slip. So Barry found it on that fatal March day. It was flood tide and pull as they might the heavily loaded boat would not answer the oars. The resistless current swept her nearer and nearer the ferry stairs at the Water Gate where a rondel, or half-moon battery, manned by English guns confronted the struggling rowers. Flustrated by the nearness of the enemy Ackerman pulled one way and big Dirck Ryckman the other while, still the remorseless flood bore them nearer and nearer the foe.

"Hollo, in the boat there! Land here and at once or we fire," came the command from the battery.

Barry, half angered and half perplexed at the scrape into which he had fallen, and with that bravado which is often born of perplexity replied to the challenge by an action which is as old as the beginning of boyhood — if we may trust the cuniform inscriptions of Assyria and the monoliths of Yucatan — he clapped his thumb to his nose and derisively waved the neighboring fingers to and fro. No self-respecting sentry could be expected to calmly stand so open and avowed a taunt. At least Corporal Hopkins of the Fusileers was not one who could and, angered by the boy's insult, he clapped his fusil-lock to his shoulder and blazed away at the boat. Quick as thought big Dirck Ryckman threw his oar before him as if to shield himself from harm, clumsier Larry Ackerman dropped flat in the bottom of the boat for safety while Barry's offending hand quitting his nose grasped Larry's deserted oar and with the energy of desperation pulled the boat's head around. Fortune favored the oarsman at last; a shore eddy caught the unwieldy craft and swung it slowly towards a point just south of the ferry stairs while a rattling fusil-lade from the half-moon battery came scattering over and around the imperilled three.

"Quick, lads; to the shore!" cried Barry excitedly; "quick or they will have us in their grip."

A clattering squad of fusileers hurried down the water-side. Big Dirck Ryckman, following nimble Barry, essayed to jump ashore, but his heavy feet striking the teetering thwarts tripped him up and sent him floundering on the beach with his feet in the water and a big fusileer sprawling atop of him. Slow-moving Larry deeming discretion the better part of valor still lay motionless at the bottom of the boat hoping that Dirck's energetic jump would shove the boat off shore and thus set him free.

But the trip and sprawl only sent the stern around and drove the boat ashore; a second fusileer grabbed the tie-rope, and Larry and the provender were prisoners. Only fleet-footed Barry, first on shore and quick of eye and wit, dodged the fore-

BARRY ESCAPES.

most pursuer and sped like the wind down the Strand and through the Winckel street heading straight for the fort while hard behind him clattered his foes. Stolid burghers too surprised to stop the fugitive, shaded their eyes and looked after the fleeing youth while the red-coated soldiers of the king as they stood on parade in the plaza fronting the fort heard the shots with wonder and thinking an engagement had begun made ready their arms for the fight. Through their lines dashed the breathless Barry. Jacob, Jr., from the mound within the fort spied him as he came and hurrying to the postern flung open the gate himself and swung it shut again right in the noses of a score of pursuers. A volley from the scarcely awakened troops rattled against the defences. Abram from the north bastion also noted the trouble and with his hot French blood surging high at the sight, he sprang straightway to the gun that commanded the English earthwork, snatched the match from the lazy gunner and with a sullen boom! the fort replied to the fusileers. As quickly, a fusee-flash on the earthwork heralded the reply. Then came a mightier flash, a sharp and thunderous explosion and the English gun bursting with its over-charge spread consternation and death behind its own embankment.

A heavy hand falls on Abram's shoulder. "What meaneth all this riot?" the Heer Leisler inquired.

"The soldiers have sought to slay Barry, Heer Governor," Abram replied, "and have even now fired on the fort."

The Governor's blood was up. "The dastards!" he cried. "This passeth my bent. Had they vented their spleen on my poor person I had not said them nay. Who am I that I would not suffer for the people. But, so long as the flag of the King's Grace flieth from this His Majesty's fort, a shot against it is foul treason against the King's High Majesty himself, and they who speed it are rebels and traitors. Hollo there, Joost Stoll," he added as that worthy with a knot of train-band men came hurrying up, "bid your match-men turn their guns on yon mud banks, and let every harquebusier stand to his arms for a sally. And do you, Ab'm, speed as you may to the Block-house on the Smits Vly and bid the Heer Brasher and the burgher-guard stand ready to support our fire. Bid him when he heareth our guns at the fort to sally forth and press the enemy in the rear as will we from the front. Thus may we trap them all and hem them safely in their quarters."

Away hurried Abram, in quick time, though secretly lest he be seen by the enemy, along the Strand to the Smits Vly, only stopping long enough on his journey to bid his mother have the Mistress Mary warned and in readiness for the sudden flight to New Rochelle. He could not yet trust himself to meet the fair girl-wife alone. But when he reached the Block-house he found a sorry sight. The Heer Brasher more discreet than valorous, hearing the guns in the town and fearful of the consequences of an engagement with the soldiers of the King deemed it wise not to resist and even as Abram hurried up he saw the burgher-guard march out without their arms and the small detachment of Major Ingolsby's troops march in. The stout log Block-house that might have withstood a long siege and held the Out Ward for the Governor was in the hands of the enemy.

" Heer Brasher," cried Abram angrily, " what meaneth this desertion of the people's cause ? "

" It meaneth safety for my neck, good *Jonkheer*," replied the over-cautious burgher. " These be the soldiers of the King's Majesty here, and it were well if Deacon Dog-driver and his aiders in the fort below did learn wisdom in time and yield to the King's guns ere they perchance may feel the King's rope. I have no stomach for a dance in the air." And the Heer Brasher hurried away,

while Abram conscious that he could not help matters here and fearful of capture if he remained
longer in the midst of Ingolsby's men hastened
back to the fort under cover of the gathering darkness and reported the sad news of the defection of
the burgher-guard to the indignant Heer Governor.

"The cravens!" he cried in wrath, striding up
and down the Governor's chamber — that very
room in which, ages ago it seemed, young Abram
had faced another angered governor — "the cravens! Let but this trouble be past and I will show
these faint-hearts who are only brave within the
smell of the chimney-corner what it is to betray
the cause of the people. *Neuswys unt koop-all**
this Heer Brasher may be, but you may call me
blaffart † if he shall not see that the people's business is the King's business — and that it were best
for him not thus to trifle with the same."

The long night passed and a new day broke on
the troubled city. The day grew to noon and still no
further move was made on either side. The train

* Nose-wise and buy-all, *i. e.*, a shrewd fellow with an eye to business
A man who comes only for the safety of Number One.
† Bully, Blusterer.

band men within the fort stood waiting the Heer
Governor's signal to make the sally; the Red-coats
behind the earthworks awaited the word to attack.
Noon passed; and there came a new summons from
the English major; " Unless the King's troops be
placed in possession of the King's fort within two
hours' time, an assault will be made and all persons
found in arms shall be adjudged as rebels and
treated as such."

" Who talketh of rebels, forsooth," said the Heer
Leisler in measured tones as his councillors gathered around him to discuss this threatening summons. " They be the rebels and not we, for are
not we the rightful government ? If what we have
done, my friends, be ill, how then came their High
Mightinesses the King and Queen to sit upon the
English throne ? For we did but act towards the
people of this loyal town even as did they towards
their realm of England. My voice is to spurn this
paper, friends. What say ye ? "

And then in solemn and impressive words, though
they knew the malice and hate of their rivals, the
council sent by the hand of their young secretary

Abram Gouverneur a ringing protest against the insulting missive of the usurping Ingolsby — a protest closing with these determined words:

"Wherefore we, not being willing to deliver ourselves and our posterity into slavery, do hereby resolve to the utmost of our power, to oppose the same by joining and assisting the Lieutenant-Governor and one another to the hazard of our lives."

Determined words, boys and girls, which almost foreshadowed and seem prophetic of the immortal Declaration that scarce a hundred years later voiced the same ringing protest against tyranny and might.

The answer was sent, and then, as the raw March day drew on towards sunset the guns of fort and battery boomed out their challenge and defiance each to each. There was a rallying of forces, a marshalling of men, a sound as of preparation on both sides to join in struggle for the mastery when, almost with the sunset, another gun boomed out upon the air; a gun that spoke neither from fort nor earthwork but further toward the sea. The watchers on the seaward ramparts of

the little fort looked off across the stretch of bay
to the low-lying curve of Nutten's Island and saw
a strange sail rounding its jagged point; they
heard the anchor chains rattle out; they saw the
sailors furl the spreading sails; and as the gun
boomed once more across the water both friend
and foe in that distracted town knew that the end
was near.   The King's Governor had arrived.

CHAPTER XXII.

MARY MEETS THE KING'S REPRESENTATIVE.

MISTRESS MARY MILBORNE sat in the ugly stone house on the Strand anxious and perplexed. Husband and father were alike in danger as none knew better than this fair child-wife of the sombre-faced Provincial secretary; for the enemies of her father had already by flattery and false representations won the newly arrived Royal Governor to their side and were determined to be bloodily revenged upon the man who for so many months had held them at bay.

The Stadt Huys bell had rung furiously, the salvos of welcoming musketry had echoed through the streets and in the council room of the Stadt Huys the Heer Governor Sloughter had taken the oath of office and listened to the complaints of the people and the charges against the Heer

Leisler. Half the town had filled the noisy streets; and the wives and daughters of the train-band men who were still inside the fort were in distress as to what might happen and loud in their grumbling against the Heer Leisler for so long defying what they now called " the King's authority."

The morning broke dull and dreary and still the restless city awaited the result of the struggle between Stadt Huys and fort. It lacked yet two hours of noon when Mary heard a well-known step on the kitchen "stoope," a familiar slamming of the half-door and speeding below caught her brother with feverish hands.

"O Jacob," she cried out, ' what news?"

"Where is the mother?" was all that Jacob, Jr., said.

Mary pushed open the door of the ample " living-room." The goode vrouw Leisler, placid as if all was well and no exciting rumors filled the air around her sat by the window calmly spinning. "Well, son?" was all she said and again came Mary's hurried inquiry "O Jacob, what news?"

" The worst news, mother," he replied, taking

his mother's hands and with a lad's clumsy effort at consolation, striving to keep a stiff upper lip even though possessed with the full sense of the importance of his information. "That *blaffart* of a Bayard is let out from his gaol; the new Governor — even when my father did acknowledge his authority, did grant him courteous welcome and did turn over to him the fort and all the King's property — hath proven himself, like all the grandees, a tyrant and a craven. He lords it in the Stadt Huys as if he were the czar of Muscovy himself, and my father the Heer Governor, the Heer Milborne, the Heer Mayor Delanoy, the Heer Doctor Beekman and all the council and — yes, Mary — Ab'm too, think of that — are apprehended as traitors to the king and lodged in the old fort gaol!"

"But sure, Jacob," cried Mary, when her brother had told his tale, "the new Governor will not dare to do so foul a thing as to keep in durance the only man who hath held the city for the King's majesty — when he doth know the truth."

"The truth; bah, Mary, you do not know him,"

said Jacob hotly; "you do not know the bloody counsels of the treacherous aristocrats and grandees that have the ear of this new Governor whom the king hath sent. Even now they are shrieking for the slaughter of my father and all the council. Gysbert Van Cortlandt did shout at me as I came from the fort with the train-bands : 'First the wolf and then the wolf's cub. So ho,' he cried to me, did he,' master jail-bird, your time will come anon !'"

"And I served him well out for it, Jacob, so did I," chuckled Barry who all hot and flushed with running now burst into the room; " and, faith, he knoweth not who did it. I tumbled him heels over head into a mud slough in the Slyck Steeger * and colored his ruffles finely. But hoy, Jacob ; 'twere best for you to get your folk away from here ; for the people — that is the grandees' following — are hot and heady, and the new Governor hath even now, so I heard at the Stadt Huys, bade the cruelest foes of the Heer Leisler prepare papers against him and his council charging them 'with traitorously levying war against the King's Majesty

* Dirty lane — now South William Street.

and with other high misdemeanors,' and the Heer Governor did bid me to say to you, goode vrouw," continued Barry, turning to Mother Leisler, "that it is his wish that you take yourself speedily to the Sieur Bonnefoy's at New Rochelle for shelter and security."

But the goode vrouw Leisler was not to be moved. "Go you, child," she said to Mary, "your life is of more value than is mine, for if your father dieth a traitor's death what is there for me to do but even to die with him — ah me, why did he ever move in this so miserable a business?"

"No, my mother," spoke up Mary warmly, "not miserable, I pray you. My father did but his duty to the people and his own brave heart and if it chanceth that the people and our Lord the King do not read his work aright, doth that make it any the less an honor for my father to have been brave and true? Ab'm hath told me" — and here a sigh as of mingled recollection and regret escaped her — "of the great admiral, the Heer Coligny, the noble captain of the Huguenots, and how he once said to his sons 'men have taken from us all they can — but there are other things than those which we see with our eyes and touch with our hands; ' and so doth it seem to me that my father, and — my husband," she added after a somewhat hesitating pause — "will be more noble even in defeat in that they have given up neither their honor nor their faith."

So they staid in the sad house on the Strand. The days sped by. On Monday the thirtieth of March the trial of the prisoners began before a band of prejudiced judges, "packed" by the malignity of their enemies and the willingness of Governor Sloughter — one of the most unjust trials that ever disgraced the legal annals of this land. Charges of treason, sedition and murder were brought against them and "for the holding by force the king's fort against the king's governor." Scant testimony in their favor was permitted and when this " insolent mockery of justice " as it has been called, was ended they were adjudged guilty, and sentence of death in the most horrible manner prescribed by the cruel old English law was pronounced against the Heer Governor Leisler and six of the eight members of his council, including also his faithful and loyal boy secretary, young Abram Gouverneur.

The tumult that followed this decision was indescribable. The city was racked with excitement. Petitions for pardon and clamors for speedy execution followed and crossed each other and so crowded upon the King's Governor that the head of that weak-minded and easily influenced man was nearly distracted with all the bother and annoyance of the affair. And so it happened that he found the cool sea breeze that, one fair April morning, played through the apple branches of the Dominie's orchard particularly restful and refreshing and he scarcely noticed that he was not alone until a gentle touch and a soft voice caused him to turn quickly.

" Might I have but a word with the Heer Governor ? " came the appealing request.

Colonel Henry Sloughter looked at the petitioner —a slight and sweet-faced girl of scarce sixteen, with fair hair and trusting blue eyes, full of appealing and anxiety. A pretty face always had an attraction for this bloated but appreciative old aristocrat.

"So girl, you wish to see the Governor, do you?" he asked.

"Yes, so please your Excellency," was the reply.

"Excellency! Don't Excellency me, child," he said, scenting a petition, "how do you know I am Excellency?"

"I know you must be, sir," replied the politic Mary — for she it was who had thus waylaid him —"for sure the Scripture saith that the Excellency is with wisdom and that wisdom giveth life, and doth not that well befit the Excellency who acteth here for the King's Gracious Majesty?"

"Ha-ha-ha; good — very good, child," laughed the flattered Governor. "Why, I protest I did not hope to find a new prophetess and so fair a one withal in this Western wilderness. Who are you, girl, and what would you with me?"

"So please your Excellency, a favor," Mary replied with a respectful courtesy.

"Ay, that will I be sworn," said the Governor with a wry twist of his red face. "'Tis in the very air of this town. What with favors and promises

GOVERNOR HENRY SLOUGHTER IS WAYLAID.

and petitions and charges I am so badgered and befooled that, odd zooks, I begin to wish I had staid quiet in sleepy Bermuda and ne'er set a foot in this seething caldron of a town. But you are a neat, trim little maiden and a clever one beside. Your favor I opine can never be a vast one. What is it, girl? Speak out."

"So please your Excellency," said Mary solemnly, "the pardon of the Heer Leisler and his fellow-prisoners."

"I thought as much," said the King's Governor, striking his cane into the soft earth. "The very children dog my steps. Why, who are you, child, and who hath put you up to this?"

"No one hath put me to it, Heer Governor, save my own prayers and desires," replied the girl. "I am Mary Milborne, and the daughter of the Heer Jacob Leisler, late Gov—"

"What, the daughter of that villain!" interrupted the surprised Governor. "Leisler's girl — and yet Milborne too — how is that? Why, sure, you are never the —"

"Yes, so please your Excellency," said Mary

with tearful eyes. "I am the unhappy child of the Heer Leisler and the equally unhappy wife of the Heer Milborne, late secretary of this Province."

"Well, body o' me," said the still surprised Governor; "this passeth my comprehension. You are but a child and yet you are —"

"A wife, your Excellency; a wife who pleadeth for her husband's pardon; a daughter who beggeth for her father's life."

"Chut, chut, girl," said the now perplexed Governor. "How can I give grace to so vile and perjured a traitor as this self-styled Governor who hath but raised turmoil in this town, who hath maltreated its worthiest citizens, and defied its lawful Master the King? So base a traitor —"

"Nay, sir, nay," broke in Mary, her belief in her father's honor getting the better of her discretion, "they be the base and villain traitors who did so malign and falsify a noble man. My father, sir, did but seek to honor and uphold the King's High Majesty against the Papists and King James's men who would have held this goodly town of ours for the old king. O sir," she said, placing her hand appealingly on the Governor's be-laced sleeve, " for the sake of his name, which hath never yet known stain; for the sake of my mother, his wife — as you, Heer Governor, have loved both mother and wife; for the sake of his children who so reverence and honor him; for the sake of the people whose cause he hath upheld — "

"The people — bah ! " broke in the fierce aristocrat to whom any reference to the rights of the people were as a red rag in the face of a bull, " who are the people, girl, that their cause should need upholding, and what cause should they have but that of their Master the King ? No, no, your petition is useless. This Leisler is a pestilent and dangerous fellow, I am well advised, and both he and Milborne have villainously and grievously oppressed this loyal city of their King. I may not wisely prejudice the decisions of their judges, and yet, I vow, child, it paineth me to see you weep so. You are vastly pretty and mightily proper and respectful withal. Never greater villains lived than those for whom you sue ; but go your ways, child, and I will see if I may not justly find other means to keep the province quiet."

So Mary left him, only partially satisfied with the outcome of her appeal. And well she might fear for the result. Each day the pressure upon the Governor grew stronger and weightier. The enemies of the Heer Leisler were determined upon his death and by fair means or foul they would have their will. They agreed to the respiting of all the prisoners except the Heer Leisler and the Heer Milborne, but when the Governor held back his signature to the death warrant for these two patriots stratagem was resorted too. A great wedding feast at the house of Colonel Bayard, Leisler's bitterest enemy, was made the occasion of the last attempt. And when, according to the habits of those hard-drinking days, the too easily tempted Governor was as the record says "drowned in his cups" — in other words disgustingly drunk — certain of the conspirators prevailed upon him to sign the cruel warrant. And so the deed was done. The enemies of the people were victorious, and ere midnight on the fourteenth of May the news went abroad. The death warrant had been signed. The Heer Governor must die.

CHAPTER XXIII.

THE deed that is so foul a stain, not only upon the annals of the city of New York, but upon the record of England's rule in her American colonies, was done. The barbarous English law specially designed for the killing of traitors — shorn of some of its barbarities, but still revolting and unjust — had been carried out. The drunken and prejudiced English Governor, appropriately named Sloughter, had yielded to the clamors of the aristocratic enemies of the only man who dared to stand for the people. The fatal death-warrant was signed, and the foes of Jacob Leisler, more ferocious than the gray wolf the boys had trapped at the bouwerie, had hastened to see the final tragedy quickly accomplished. This record, devoted to the culture of gentle thoughts in the young, may not be used to conjure up this final picture of vindictive hate and of brutal revenge. It is sufficient to say that on Saturday, May 16, 1691, on what was called the Commons, just east of where now are Park Row and the post-office, and in the midst of a pelting rain as if the very heavens were weeping over the crime, the Heer Jacob Leisler met his fate like the brave and manly man he was.

Hurried over in our histories, unrecorded in most of our works of reference, unknown to the majority of those to whom it should be familiar, and unnoticed in the very city where the memory of the man should be most honored, the life-story of Jacob Leisler is one that should shine on the pages of American history and be familiar to American youth. The man who dared all for freedom, the first to stand for the majesty of the people, the earliest of American patriots, his story is one which in this far too selfish world of ours should not be lightly passed over, or carelessly forgotten.

With him, too, died Jacob Milborne. Moody, taciturn, revengeful and grasping, his friends were but few and his influence upon the quick-tempered

Heer Governor was one cause of downfall. Had he but counselled moderation where he advised severity, the friends of the Heer Governor would have increased instead of lessened, and fair Mistress Mary would neither have been wife nor widow while yet only a sweet young girl.

Under the old theory that the sins of the fathers must be visited on the children even to the third and fourth generation, the old English law of attainder, both cruel and unjust, declared the wife and children of the Heer Leisler as outcasts. His property was confiscated and, bowed already under the shadow of his unjust death, those who were dearest to him were stripped of their rights and possessions.

In the fort the six members of the Heer Leisler's council still lay under sentence of death — a sentence which neither Governor Sloughter, nor his successor Ingolsby * dared carry out — for already the reaction that followed the murder of the Heer Leisler was stirring the justice lovers of old New York.

* Governor Sloughter died suddenly in July, 1691, only two months after the execution of the men he allowed to be murdered by their enemies, and Major Ingolsby succeeded, temporarily, to his office.

At last young Barry Van Schaick, chafing and restless under this delay of justice, and anxious to do something that should relieve his friends, formed the desperate resolution to help Abram escape from jail. And, casting about for help, he bethought himself of Abram's old friends, the Indian sakemackers at Aspatong. So, one fair August morning Barry set out for a consultation with Katonah and Papaig ; but as he drew near the Wedding Place where he was to cross to the Westchester side, he suddenly recalled the slight unpleasantness with the ferryman's wife, already described in these pages. The Heer Leisler's wrath had fallen heavily upon them for that action, and Barry knew that the ferryman's wife was no friend of his.

But, as he turned up the Harlem bank to find some other means of crossing, he suddenly heard a loud cry for help. Looking in the direction indicated, he saw a small boat, evidently fast filling with water, and drifting toward the Sound, while in the boat, hatless and oarless, a clerical-looking figure was appealing for help.

" 'Tis Cose Verveelen's leaky boat," said Barry,

"and, good faith, the dominie, if such he be who is within it, is like to be food for fishes speedily, unless"—

But by the time he had finished the sentence he was out of his clothes and in the water, swimming straight for the foundering craft which, once reached, he pushed to shore, and then helped the stranger out.

"Now, praise to heaven and thanks to you, good youth, valiant youth," said the relieved dominie when once his feet struck *terra firma*. "I did but seek to fare across the river, leaving my good steed tethered on the further shore till I could rouse some one to set him across, for none appeared in sight, and the ferry horn seemeth lost. And when I essayed to push over in this boat, behold it was full of water, and I was in sorry plight from which your kindly offices did save me. Verily they that go down to the sea in ships — or even smaller craft — do suffer chance, as Holy Writ doth say. Twice thus in your goodly town have I now been in sore peril and been safely delivered."

"Twice, said you, reverend sir?" said Barry, now nearly in his clothes again.

"Ay, good youth, twice said I," replied the dominie. "For the other peril was some three years agone when from a tree-top, in what you term the Dominie's Orchard, a ravening wolf did well nigh " —

Barry burst out laughing.

"Why, so 'tis good Dominie Woolley, is it not?" he said; "the same whom Ab'm Gouverneur did deliver from peril, when he knocked down the bear from the Dahrklaashaa in the Dominie's Orchard. Yes, yes, I mind it now. Poor Ab'm!"

"Poor, said you, good youth? And why poor?" queried our old friend, good Parson Woolley, met in New York again after a long stay in Boston town. "What harm hath befallen that brave youth?"

"Harm, reverend sir?" said Barry sadly; "the worst of harm. For is he not even now in the fort-jail under sentence of death?"

"Death?" echoed Parson Woolley. "Why, why, what evil hath he done?"

"None, reverend sir, save to stand up for the people in our late trouble, and to be the Heer Governor's secretary — the Heer Leisler's, I mean."

"That lad!" exclaimed Parson Woolley in surprise. " Surely, my friend Ab'm of the bear-orchard is not that same wise Abraham Gouverneur whose praise was in all folks' mouths at Boston town, and who suffers imprisonment with the rest of Mr. Leisler's council?"

" It is even he, reverend sir," replied Barry sadly.

" Why, this passeth comprehension," said the English parson. "And he is to die for treason, you say? Surely blood enow hath been spilt in this miserable business without taking this young lad's life. Truly the slaughter of my good friend Mr. Leisler should satisfy his enemies. And I would that I could help my young friend of the orchard —in truth I do. Let me see. Why might we not ask justice from the King's majesty—"

" The King," cried Barry, "but how?"

" Softly; fair and softly, good youth," said Parson Woolley, deep in thought. " Here hath been revenge enow, but not justice. Did not the worshipful and reverend Mr. Increase Mather say but last week in Boston town while we were in converse upon this very theme that Mr. Leisler had been most barbarously murdered and that he would gladly aid his family in their plea for pardon from the King's Grace?   But whom could we send before his Highness?"

"Ab'm, if he were out of gaol," said Barry without hesitation, "or why not Jacob, Jr., reverend sir — Jacob, Jr., the Heer Gov —— the Heer Leisler's son?   He is a rare pleader, reverend sir."

Parson Woolley nodded.   "Mayhap 'tis the very thing," he said.   "The King's Majesty is said to be fair and well-minded toward the right, and this young man might win where a grave and alien man might not.   We must consider this.   For mayhap 'twill thus save our good friend, Abraham, from death.   And our other little friend — the worthy Mr. Leisler's fair young daughter — how is she?"

"The widow Milborne is well in body, but not in spirit, reverend sir," answered Barry gravely.

"Nay, I asked not of any Madame Milborne," said Parson Woolley; "I did but inquire after the little maid who was with young Abraham in the orchard — the fair young maiden, Mary Leisler."

"She is the widow Milborne, reverend sir,"

answered Barry, "as none knoweth better than Ab'm and myself." And he heaved a sigh that told of much change in mind since the day when he had grumbled because Mary must go with them on some boyish excursion.

The good parson was more surprised than ever at this piece of information, and when Barry had told him all the sorry story he grew still more determined to help the lads, and next day at the goode vrouw Weber's quiet cottage on the Kolch — for they dared not meet anywhere in the town openly — Barry and Jacob, Jr., after consultation with Parson Woolley, decided that Jacob should try his power of personal pleading.

And so, in the early fall of 1691, Jacob, Jr., was spirited away to Boston where Doctor Increase Mather and other prominent men interested themselves in his case. Barry's plan of deliverance for Abram was also carried out, though not in the way he had intended; for in the spring of 1692 Abram escaped in a fishing boat to Boston. There the well-known Sir William Phipps interested himself in the lads. They were sent to London with letters to the Massachusetts agents there. But, while thankful to the friends who for the Heer Leisler's sake, and to do justice to his memory, had enabled them to lay their case before the King, the boys themselves, now fast becoming men, had bound themselves together by a solemn vow to "rest not, neither to waver in their efforts, come defeat, come distress, come persecution even, until they had withdrawn from the Heer Governor Leisler and his family the stain and taint of the lying charge of treason."

It was a heritage of work, but brave lads in every age have brought victory out of darkness and defeat. Pluck and manliness are sure to win the day.

CHAPTER XXIV.

IT was a fair May morning in the spring of 1695. The young vrouw Mary Milborne stood at her window in the old stone house on the Strand breathing in all the beauty and glory of the early spring and looked across the dancing river to the Breucklen hills, thinking of the wide ocean that lay beyond and how, thousands of miles away, her brother Jacob and Abram Gouverneur still strove for justice from the English King.

The four years that had passed since that sad May morning of 1691 had brought a fresher and fairer bloom to her cheek for, even in the midst of sorrows, youth and health will assert themselves. The fair child-wife of fifteen was now the blooming young woman of nineteen. And as she stood thus by her open window, deep in thought, she recalled that day four years ago when on the Commons beyond the city walls husband and father had both been taken from her.

"I will go down and bide with the mother," she said; "for sure this day is the darkest in all the year to her."

But even as her foot touched the lower stair the door flew open and in burst with scant ceremony young Barry Van Schaick, now assistant to Joost Stoll at the tan yard and the store in the Winckel street, which had once been the Heer Leisler's.

"Tidings, tidings, Mary!" he cried — he never had, and he vowed he never would, call her the widow Milborne or the goode vrouw; vrouw indeed, he would say, she who has scarce had time to be even a fraulein! "Tidings, Mary," he cried; "here is Garry Ten Eyck all the way from the great dock * and Teuny Fever-foot from De Reimer's well † both with news that *The Great Christopher* is rounding Nutten Island and will be at the great dock with this flood, before the hour is out."

---

* The great dock of the city in 1695 extended from the present Coenties slip to Whitehall street.

† One of the public wells in Broad street near the bridge across the canal.

A FAIR MAY MORNING.

" *The Great Christopher!* " exclaimed Mary, " why, Barry, that is Ab'm Staat's brigantine, is it not ? "

Barry nodded assent.

" Then sure he will have news of Jacob, Jr.," said Mary, " and of " —

" Yes, and of Ab'm too," said Barry, rounding out Mary's statement, while she went on hastily :

" And perchance not only news of Jacob, but — "

" But Jacob's self, as well," came a cheery voice from the doorway, and Mary was clasped in her brother's arms, while Barry, who had planned this surprise, as his custom was, hugged himself for very joy in the hallway.

" Why, Jacob," cried Mary, the glow of pleasure and the flush of surprise playing across her fair cheek, " and is it you — really and truly you ? And what tidings do you bring me ? "

" Surely, it is really and truly I, sister mine," said Jacob gleefully, " and with great and joyous tidings too; but where is the mother ? "

Mother Leisler had heard the commotion and her son soon bent for her blessing and her welcoming kiss, while all were speedily listening to the story of the loyal son who through nearly four years of anxiety, disappointment and doubt held fast to his duty and reclaimed the name and possessions of his martyred father from the taint of treason and the ban of royal displeasure.

But, almost in the very midst of this story, and while Jacob was detailing his adventures and how largely through Abram's tact and good management, he had won first the friendship and then the open aid of the courtly and noble Lord Bellomont, the friend of the king, Mary broke in with, "And Ab'm; why, where *is* Ab'm, Jacob?"

"Trust me he is not far behind," said Barry with laughter-filled eyes, and Jacob added, "no, not far, Mary; he did but tarry to see his mother awhile ere he made his greetings here to you; and by this time —"

"By this time," cried mischievous Barry, "he should be just where he is I'll be bound — without the kitchen door there, fearful, as of old, lest he scratch up mother Leisler's sanded floor," and Barry threw open the broad half-door.

Sure enough there stood Abram on the kitchen

"stoope," brave as was Jacob in ruffles and velvet and hose, as grand and noble-looking, Barry declared, as any Royal Governor that ever strutted at the Fort.

They dragged him in, despite mother Leisler's sanded floor, and after these new greetings and congratulations were over, Abram and Jacob, jointly and with many interruptions from their eager listeners, concluded the story of the their heritage of work ; how, with determination never faltering, and courage high and strong despite all enemies and obstacles — before lords and council, before judges and royal ministers and even before the King's majesty himself they had plead for justice; had made first friends, and then adherents and advocates and, conquering all opposition, had secured in April, 1695, "a reversal of the attainder of Captain Leisler, Mr. Milborne, and Mr. Gouverneur " and a full pardon for all political offences (which were not offences at all, Barry declared) and a restitution of confiscated property, thus freeing the name and estate of the murdered governor and his counsellors from all stain of treason and of loss.

And as they finished their recital Abram said to Mary in solemn and earnest tone,

"Well, *belle* Marie, have we not kept our vow?"

"Ay, truly you have, brothers both," said Mary, laying a hand on the arm of each — "and to you belongs our loving duty and our duteous loves as to those who save even from distress and death."

But the trouble that is ever the heritage of injustice and wrong-doing was by no means ended with this brilliant victory of these two brave-hearted lads. For many a year the quarrels and bickerings that grew out of the Leisler persecution agitated and distracted this little city of scarce five thousand inhabitants. "Leisler" and "anti-Leisler" were for years the opposing parties that swayed the city politics, made the lines of Royal Governors miserable and were the chief burden to the mayors of the town.

One by one also the bitterest foes of the murdered governor found out that "the way of the transgressor is hard." The worshipful Heer Van Cortlandt died with the shadow of embezzlement hanging over him in 1701, and the Heer Colonel

Bayard lived to be himself tried and convicted of
high treason, to be saved from the gallows only by
the death of King William and the incoming of a

new reign, but not until his "dutiful" children had
conspired to request his punishment so that they
might be freed from the expenses of his trial and
succeed to his property!

But long before these political troubles grew to
be so hot and bitter there came a fair spring morn-

ing in the year 1699 when, with much rustle and stateliness, with silks and velvets, silver and gold, scarfs and laces, wigs and buckles and all the elegance of old-fashioned colonial array, a bridal train swept up to the low stoop of the little Dutch church on Garden Alley* and in through the narrow doorway to where in sounding and solemn Dutch ways and phrase Dominie Du Bois read the marriage service. And while Parson Woolley beamed benignantly through his big-bowed spectacles, and while Barry Van Schaick was one great and continuous smile, and old Joost Stoll relaxed his stolid face, and mother Leisler smiled even through her tears ; while from the Royal Governor, Lord Bellomont, down to Teuny Fever-foot, the Indian runner, all the old city — save the bitter anti-Leislerians — came with good wishes and congratulations, the Abram and Mary of the childish days of the Dominie's Orchard, the wolf trap and the wall, became at last the worshipful Heer and Madame Abram Gouverneur.

Thus our story that has been so shadowed by

* Garden Alley — afterwards Garden Street and now Exchange Place

tragedy closes amid the merry clangor of wedding bells that are historic. These two who had been playfellows from childhood, and friends through all the trials and troubles of later years, now in their young manhood and womanhood, started on a long and loving life-journey. And from their happy union sprang a line of worthy American men and women who have kept green the memory of that first of American patriots to whom they can proudly trace their ancestral line ; and whose names have been counted among the honored ones of the city that has grown so strong and mighty since those far-off days of two centuries back when from the Copake rocks and the fort to the Land Gate and the Horse mill, the little Dutch city was full of the struggle and turmoil, the plotting and planning that made the town historic and brought so much of pleasure and of pain to little Mistress Mary, the Governor's daughter, in that eventful epoch known as " Leisler's times."

THE END.